ISBN: 9798296967527

Published by Russell Jones

Imprint: Independently published

First edition, 2025

Cover and interior design by Russell Jones

Made available worldwide in ebook, hardback and paperback via Kindle Direct Publishing

RUSSELL JONES

BABY'S BREATH

For Mel, without whom...

Contents

Chapter 1: The Flowers

There was still blood on my arm when I got home. Nobody had noticed. Why would they? I'd watched my clothes being taken away in sealed boxes. There was blood enough.

Thoughts came out wrong, if they came at all. Time was wrecked, and places too. Nothing followed, nothing flowed. The hospital was only ten minutes from the school gates, but it had taken me—what?—hours. It was dark when I arrived anyway, and I was so shook I couldn't remember if they'd given me the sedative before or after the cop had visited the ambulance. "What's your name, hon?" he'd asked, his features arranged just so. He had to make that face, tell me he was sorry for my loss, repeat my name back to me. This was his script.

"What's your date of birth, Erin? What's your address, Erin? Do you want us to inform anybody that you're okay, Erin?"

Oh, I'm okay, am I? Then why is this paramedic wiping blood off me?

He didn't ask which of the children had died. Maybe he didn't want me thinking about it. I wish.

After that, I was driven out towards Columbus in a hail of sirens, and then the world blinked and I was suddenly in a curtained room that reeked of lemon-scrubbed fear trying to pass as hygiene, with somebody hooking a fresh drip into my arm.

Don't even ask who told me they needed my clothes as evidence. All I know is: an orderly delivered a heap of shapeless garments donated to the hospital chaplaincy. Some dead man's sweatpants with a cigarette hole burned in the thigh. I stuck my pinky through it and thought about a hole the same size in Della Morrison. She'd been so close that her blood had set on my shirt, sticky as old syrup.

I stripped. Changed. A tech with an ID badge came in and started boxing up my clothes.

"I thought you used plastic bags?"

She didn't look up. "For clothes, we use cardboard. Plastic sweats, and then you get condensation. It can ruin the blood pattern. You get mold too."

When she was done, she gazed at me, flat, like she couldn't figure out why I wasn't crying. *You and me both, sister.* It seemed like a moment when I should. Maybe the drip explained it.

Later—who knows how much later—I was discharged into an Uber paid for by the state. The hospital staff had been too busy, I hadn't seen a mirror, and my kindly, solicitous driver sized me up of me straight away and gave me silence. So nobody told me I still had blood on me. It wasn't until I got home, picked up the rain-soaked flowers left by some well-wisher, and lifted my key to the door. That's when I saw it. My arm. The dried spatter.

In movies, traumatized people knock back bourbon or slump fully dressed in the shower. Me, I dropped the wet flowers on the floor in the hallway and simply stared, already trying to build a levee around myself. Anything to hold back the flood. What I felt was too deep, too dangerous to be allowed loose. I focused instead on that checkout-register tone right at the edge of hearing, incessant in my ears. Nobody tells you how loud a handgun is in an enclosed space. Movies get that wrong too.

I felt like somebody had shuffled my brain. Let me stop, slow down, place events in order again.

First came the shooting.

Then the running and the ambulance.

Whatever had come before all of that had gotten washed away in a torrent of panic. Other than my name and the noise, all I could tell the cops that night was what came after, and they already knew that much. They'd been there, or just about.

I'd made it out of the school grounds into the arms of a uniformed kid, younger than me anyway, first on the scene and sprinting madly ahead of his older partner. He caught me, and we raced bent double along Mill Hollow, towards a rapidly gathering forest of flashing blue lights. I got bundled into an ambulance the second it arrived, and we played my first game of Repeat Erin's Name. Maybe it's just how officials are trained.

"I need to examine you for injuries, Erin. Does anywhere hurt, Erin? You're doing fine, Erin."

Hearing my name spoken over and over again, it felt like a chant, a mantra, like I'd accidentally started a cult. The pasted-on, feel-nothing smiles from the ambulance crew didn't help. *You're one of the lucky ones*—that's what it was selling. *All this blood isn't yours.*

I didn't want to think whose it was. Plenty was Della Morrison's, I knew that much. Other kids were alive—I'd seen them run—but 400 children go to Cedar Ridge Elementary, and I knew the fates of perhaps ten. Then instinct had dragged me away from danger.

But what about that other instinct, the one that tells you you're supposed to stay with children? The one I should have had all along.

"How we doing?"

That cop, the older one, was standing on the sidewalk at the back of the ambulance, his hat in his hand. I'd seen him on Mill Hollow too. Did he help to save me? Could've. Didn't remember. Didn't know how to reply either: that I'm unharmed, apparently, so why can't I make my brain work right?

The cop heaved himself into the back and bent low to look into my eyes.

"You did nothing wrong, you hear me."

Yeah? A half hour ago I abandoned dying kids, so fuck you, badge. He put a steadying hand on my shoulder. "Detectives and the BCI are gonna want to talk to you, but not today. Here's my card. You call me if you need anything."

It all began—what—ten hours ago? Twelve? And now I was home, where time was meant to be one thing after another, like normal. But here I was, frozen in the hallway, a statue in grief-sweats from the tragedy bin, my own clothes tagged and boxed as evidence. How could anything be normal again?

My heart was still tuned to go off at every sound, so the rap on the door left me scrambling to breathe before I could get it together enough to peer through the peephole. Eddie, in his shirtsleeves in the middle of the night. Had he been sitting in his car, waiting?

"Shit."

He must've heard that. "Hey," he called, keeping his voice low. "You okay?"

I had to let him in. What was I gonna do—fake sleep? I opened the door.

"Hey," he said again. "I saw it on the news."

In that small space, his bulk crowded me. I backed against the wall, shaking again, even though he was making a face to show he cared. He must have looked up how to do it before he drove over. Or copied it from a dog.

"You been smoking."

"Jesus, is that your big problem?"

"No, no—I just… Look, I was worried, alright?"

I shook my head. *Who isn't?*

He stood there like he was waiting for a fresh script to appear. "They had you on Channel 9, from some guy's phone."

Great. Way to be famous.

He took a step back and assessed the problem, as he saw it. I heard my mom's voice: *The Lord sees effort*, as he started again. "I can't even… I mean, fuck, Helen, I can't imagine what it was like. I just wanted to see you. Make sure you're okay."

"What the hell are you doing here, Eddie?"

"Like I said, I saw you on the news. You were all bloody, and I—I just needed to see you. Make sure you're okay." He shrugged. "You matter to me."

"I matter to you," I repeated back at him. *Jesus.* I closed my eyes, so I didn't have to watch him test-driving emotions.

"I get it," he said. "I get we're not a thing or whatever. I'm not an idiot."

"You're idiot enough to believe whoever told you you're not an idiot."

In the silence that followed, that small line appeared between his brows.

"So... you're not Helen Calley. You're Erin Callahan. That's what they said on the news."

I spread my arms to show the blood. "Are you kidding me right now? That's what you wanna talk about?"

"I'm here for you at three in the morning, and you didn't even tell me your right name!"

I opened the door, then slammed it behind him. He shouted that I was a bitch from the walkway. I shouted that he was a dick to the empty hall, then I picked up the flowers and shook my head at them: *can you believe this guy?*

In the yellow dresser I found an ancient vape, and thanked whichever God had been off duty today that it had some charge left. Barely any flavor, like sucking on an old candy wrapper, but at least it was less of a personal failure than finding a bottle. *Yay me.* I drew on it a few times, then shoved it into my pocket. My fingers grazed something small.

I pulled out the card the cop had given me. Officer Mark Kessler, it said, and on the back, in a tight, crabbed hand, a case number and: Call if you need me, followed by his direct line. What was it he'd said? That I'd have a visit from detectives and…? someone else, some other capital-letter agency. It wasn't the FBI, it was…

I didn't want to look it up, didn't want to know. But my hands knew my mind was screwed, and they'd taken over, handling things before my brain could interrupt.

They reached for my phone and I saw Eddie had WhatsApped me maybe a hundred times. There were messages from Ty and a half-dozen other names, even one from Danny Krawczyk, probably parked at some roadside diner a thousand miles from here. Sixteen missed calls from Mom. Was that a new record? I wasn't calling back—not now. She had a way of clawing at memories until they bled, and I was already remembering too much.

A small fist wrapped around my skirt.

"Miss Callahan?" Della's voice, clear as a bell in my head.

Then the other memory, the one I kept trying to push away. The red hoodie in the doorway. He'd pushed up his sleeves to the elbow, like he was getting down to work. My thumb, desperately mashing 9-1-1 on the screen. The door opening before I could hit send.

I'd flung the phone at him. It hit him hard, on the bare skin of his forearm. Fucker didn't even look at me. Just raised his gun.

I squeezed my eyes shut, trying to banish the picture.

Think of something else. Think about the problem at hand.

So I Googled: *who questions you after a school shooting?*

The Ohio Bureau of Criminal Investigation. BCI. That's what Kessler had said.

This was better. Tasks.

Tasks are easier than feelings.

I spent an hour digging. *Do I get my clothes back? How long does the investigation take?* And—this one mattered, because my head was still leaking from the seams—*What happens if I don't answer questions?*

I dropped my phone when it vibrated in my hand. Another message from Mom. *"Pick up. We're all praying for you."*

Nothing from Dad, of course.

I needed another chore, anything to keep my hands busy, anything to keep my mind off my mind. My eyes drifted around the room—the garbage, the folded pile of laundry—and then they landed on the flowers I'd dumped on the kitchen counter after Eddie left.

Gerbera daisies and baby's breath in fancy-ass wrapping, their stems probably crushed now, dripping rainwater. Just another mess I'd have to clean up. I didn't even know if I owned a vase. I'd just stick them in the sink for now. The ribbons were already limp, the cellophane smeared with dirt, and tucked deep inside the wrapping was a small, plain white card. I almost missed it. Probably just a generic note from a well-wisher. *Thinking of you.* Perfect. Fucking. Timing.

I held the bouquet over the sink and pulled the card free. Crisp and stiff, as impersonal as a receipt—

small, square, plain.

No name. Just five printed words.

The air punched from my lungs and my stomach bottomed out.

"I killed them for you."

Baby's Breath

Chapter 2: The Invasion

That's another thing movies get wrong: nobody ever just calls the cops.

Well screw that. You never saw anybody dial 9-1-1 quicker. I'd have broken even more records if my hands weren't shaking so badly that it took me three tries to get the numbers right.

"9-1-1, what is your emergency?"

The dispatcher's voice was flat, bored, and a million miles away. She took my report like this kind of thing happened all the time, like somebody had vandalized my gate or dinged my car. Yet more corporate repetition of my name: "Lock the door, Erin. Wait for the officers to arrive, Erin." As if I hadn't already slammed every deadbolt home, as if I hadn't considered pushing the dresser against the door.

I'd dropped the card as soon as I saw it—those five words could have burned a hole in my hand. But I could still see it on the counter, from my new position on the kitchen floor. I closed my eyes and found I was gasping for air, my pulse pounding, the terror a cold flood rising. That crushing, sinking, drowning feeling. Every creak of the old house was him, whoever the hell he was, coming back to finish the job. Outside, the night was a wall of impenetrable black, and inside I'd slammed my eyes shut like a child avoiding a nightmare.

"Miss Callahan?"

Not now.

"Miss Calley?"

A small hand tugging at my skirt. Della's voice in my head.

"I'm scared."

Bang. Bang. Bang.

The sound made me leap. My doorbell had been busted for months. Neighbors, when they tapped at all, tapped soft for parcel deliveries, loud when it was two in the goddamn morning already. But this banging was different—an official, two-handed, uniformed thump.

Dawn was nudging in—gray and wet, as though the world had started over without me. I crawled to the door and squinted through the peephole to see a pair of plainclothes cops, one of them holding up a badge in the growing light. He was two steps ahead of the other, but stepped back to let her speak when

I opened the door.

"Erin Callahan?" she said, as though the world hadn't gone to hell since I last slept. "Fairfield County Sheriff's Office. I'm Detective Lomax and this is—"

She was neat and tight, solid in her gray pantsuit. I immediately forgot the name of her partner, the one with the glasses and a careful, contained face.

"We're very sorry for your loss," he said.

"Our condolences," she added. "May we come in?"

I picked the chair next to the dresser that I never use because it's not comfortable. I'd forgotten how upright it made me. She made three instant coffees, and without comment moved a *Marie Claire* off the sofa so her partner could sit. He didn't. He didn't even look at me, he just got out a notebook and placed it beside the flowers and the card on the kitchen counter, and started with his phone and his blue plastic gloves, turning the bouquet to capture every angle, landscape and portrait.

"Miss Callahan," she began, leaving Glasses to do his work. "It was a terrible thing, what happened yesterday. We're all reeling, everybody. It's hit the whole community."

She talked in soft-edged pieces, leaving gaps in conversation for others to fill. But right now I had nothing to contribute to what the whole community felt, so there was just silence.

"We're working under Major Brenner out of Lancaster Division of Police, and I'm responsible for collecting witness statements. In time you'll likely hear from other agencies—crisis response, counseling and so on. And in the next hour the forensics team will arrive here to do a study of... of the delivery you received. But we have an active investigation right now. We need to move quickly, so we can't wait for them. I hope you understand. Can we call you Erin?"

Sure.

"Okay Erin. Let's start with the basics. Are you okay?"

I laughed dryly. *No.*

She nodded. "You will be." She left another space. "You don't know who sent you these flowers?"

I shook my head.

"And you have no idea why?"

"I mean—he says, on the card..." I pointed to the flowers, as though they might have forgotten about them. She nodded again, keeping it slow, letting my pulse ease off, letting her calm wrap around me.

"He? You think: the shooter?"

I glared at her: "Who else was it going to be?"

She nodded. "We understand there was a single shooter?"

"I only saw one."

"That's what we think, too. We think he managed to exit the school before our units entered the building. Now I know this is hard, but can you help us build a picture of him?"

I closed my eyes, trying to see it and trying not to look at the same time. "He wasn't Black." *Who is around here?* "Not Mexican either. Latino. Not that." Not fat, not skinny. Not tall or short. Not old or young. In my telling, my classroom was destroyed by somebody with no features whatsoever. He'd worn a scarf up over his nose, like he was about to knock over a stagecoach, not a school. To me, he was just a shape with a gun and a face he didn't want me to see.

Lomax paused and decided to start again, to keep things simple.

"How was he dressed?"

"He had—yeah, a red shirt. Like, a faded red. It was real big, long on him."

"Anything written on it?"

I shook my head: no idea.

"What about his hair?"

"I—I don't know." Glasses didn't look up from his forensic photoshoot, he just asked: "Bald?"

"No, no—" I was excited now, I had something. "He had a hood up. His top was a hoodie, like an oversize one. Red oversized hoodie. I couldn't see his hair—I'm sorry, I'm trying."

"You're doing great," said Lomax.

I am, aren't I? I remembered one thing, and that wasn't the thing you asked about. Whoop.

"Did you interact with him at all?"

"Hold on, wait, I have my own questions here. Do you know—do you know the names of anybody yet?"

"The victims?" Lomax said, gently. "I'm so sorry Erin, we're still collecting details. And specialist officers are still working with the families. We can't release any information yet."

I sat back and looked at the ceiling in silence. Glasses moved beside Lomax, glanced at his notes, and picked up the thread. "The last question was: did you interact with the shooter at all?"

"Not really, no."

"Is that 'No'?"

"I mean… not really, I just—I hit him and then he started shooting and—"

"Hold on, you *hit* him?"

"With my phone, I was trying to—"

"You hit him with your phone?" Glasses asked. "*That* phone? Right there?"

They both leaned toward it on the table. Lomax nodded to Glasses. "We'll have to take this into property."

"Wait, what—? No, hold on, I need that."

"Write her a receipt, Demko." *Alex Demko: that was Glasses, that's how she'd introduced him.* He lifted it like it was a live grenade and began working it into an evidence bag.

"But that's my phone," I told her. "I'll lose all my messages, my contacts."

"They're stored on the cloud," she said. "You can just download them again."

"Oh, great. I'll just download them onto the imaginary phone I keep in my ass."

"What's the passcode?" said Demko. "Saves time."

I winced. 0-1-0-4. My birthday. He made a note again while Lomax pressed the button on the side through the plastic bag and looked carefully at the screen. "You have a lot of missed messages. Mostly your mom."

Expressionless Demko raised his eyebrows.

I looked down. My hands were knotted in my lap, so I made them lie flat. My fingers had gone white. When I looked up again the room was charged with the kind of stillness that waits to bite.

"Do you know your mom's number," Lomax asked, "so you can call from another phone?"

"Of course I do." *It's on a sticker inside the cover of one of the Bibles she gave me. Close enough, right?*

"Okay, good. So. Let's go through the timeline, so I have it straight. Did you hear anything strange before he came in your classroom?"

"What, like noises? I heard some shouting and then it was, like, boom, straight away, shooting."

"He was shooting up your room?"

"No, next door, in Caterpillar. Steve Dublin's room. Stephen with a P-H." *Dead.*

"Got it," said Demko.

"What's your class called?" asked Lomax.

"Lightning Bugs." *Dead. Dead. Dead.* But the sympathy in her eyes was a foothold. I could keep going.

"And then what?"

"Well—it went quiet for a moment. Or no shooting, anyway. I got the kids under the tables. I grabbed my phone—I was gonna call you guys. And the next thing, he came into my room and—"

The hammering on the door was so loud it felt like it was coming through the wall. Demko was on his feet before I could react. He opened the door to a group of uniformed cops and lab coats carrying silver briefcases. He nodded at them, then turned to us. "They've got the warrant."

Lomax stood. "The team is here to do a full forensic sweep of the house, Erin. It's standard procedure."

It didn't feel standard. It felt like an invasion. They moved through my space with quiet gloves and sharp eyes, their presence turning my home—turning my life—into a crime scene.

I watched them from the kitchen, stranded behind the U-shaped counter as they took over the room. One of them dusted the narrow hallway, his movements so precise he didn't even brush the wall on his way to the dark staircase. Another catalogued the living area, his gaze sweeping over the overflowing bookcases where takeout menus were now potential exhibits, filed between the paperbacks I hadn't read.

Go on, dust the unpaid bills. Take my student debt into custody, and see if you can make it die falling down the stairs.

Even my one point of pride, the dresser I'd painstakingly refurbished in a defiant splash of yellow, took on the status of a suspect, its surface photographed from three different angles like a mugshot. They documented the stiff, upright chair beside it. They photographed the only picture I had of my dad—a metal frame around me aged about fourteen, and him in a checked shirt, faded yellow by the sun, by some blurry lakeside.

From there, they moved into a detailed audit of a sofa whose springs had long surrendered, buried under a woven gray throw I found in a thrift store, picked ragged by some other woman's cat. God knows what revelations they thought I'd stuffed down there. The only bright spot was when one of the techs nudged the IKEA lamp and—as it always does—it sagged slowly to a drunken angle. I watched in quiet triumph as he battled to right it again. *Not so easy, is it?*

They took the flowers, the card, my fingerprints, and a DNA swab. They catalogued the thin curtains at the front and sampled the cheap plastic blinds at the back, while I tried to pretend nobody here was aware of the smell of dust. Outside, two guys were taking details of nearby CCTV cameras, their search extending into the weed-choked patch of dirt I called a garden. They even cleared my overflowing garbage. For a second, I thought they were helping me to tidy up. Turns out that was just more evidence.

I stood in a fast-flowing river, watching pieces of my life—the sad, the messy, the private—get swept away in Ziplock and latex. And then, as quickly as they'd arrived, they were all gone. The forensic coats filed out without a word. Demko managed a clipped, "Take care," without making eye contact. Lomax did it for both of them, holding my gaze for a second, before adding, "Look after yourself. We'll be in touch."

Then they moved on to the next job. To the next screwed-up life.

What was left for me? A mess. Heartache. And a fucked-up, three-way orgy of guilt: For somehow provoking the shooting. For surviving it. For not understanding a damn thing.

All I know is they are dead, and I am unharmed.

That's what they tell me. *Unharmed.*

That's really what they said.

So now I was alone, left with the simple job of putting myself back together. Too numb to cry, too frozen to tremble, but somehow it was my job to rebuild everything. Every time I tried to get a handle on what had happened to me, it changed form— too close to focus on, then too distant to see. Too sharp to touch, then too blunt to be real. Too dark to unravel, then so bright it burned.

So instead, I looked at the house and started thinking in practical steps. Hands, not heart.

I'd love to say the cops had trashed the place— but I'd already been doing a pretty solid job of that on my own. If anything, they'd done me a favor. Drawers I'd meant to clear out forever were suddenly wide open. I spent the rest of the morning filling Hefty bags, and by the end of it, the place looked better than it had in years.

And the busywork gave me just enough clarity to start shaping a plan. Plans and tasks—that's what you do when your head's been scraped raw. You keep your hands busy so the thoughts don't settle.

I didn't know what I was aiming for. Survival, maybe. And a job. The school would need someone to blame, and until the manhunt turned something up, paraprofessionals were the bottom-shelf. Cheap. Disposable. Cannon fodder for the outrage machine. I had to get ahead of it. Call Principal Greevy, remind her I was still human.

Except my phone was gone, bagged and tagged. My car was still behind yellow police tape.

So I needed a multi-step plan.

And step one meant getting into character.

Baby's Breath

Chapter 3: The Watcher

I packed a bag with the clothes I'd need for Mom, then spent an hour in front of the mirror, patching the cracks in the facade, faking eight hours of sleep and a life where I wasn't the girl the police were circling because she gets *Congratulations-On-Your-Massacre* flowers.

The goal: look hot, look effortless, look like the other me. The one guys knew as "Helen", who walks into a man's house like she still has something he wants. Ty Holcomb had wanted that thing plenty. Maybe he wouldn't be thrilled to see me turn up at his workplace, but it was better than showing up at his home, and I was pretty sure I could talk him into handing over the keys to a truck.

I peeked through the window. The media had got to the school only ten minutes after cops arrived, and hit the hospital right after that. Safe bet they'd be scouting for survivors to put on camera. But there was nothing outside, just East 6th in all her glory: a cat's cradle of power lines strung over narrow houses on plots that were more crabgrass than green. Vinyl siding and sagging porches, and families stuffing their problems into trash cans already begging for mercy.

But no branded news van with a dish. Guess I wasn't today's tragedy. This might even work.

It stopped working straight away. I was still locking my door when I heard a voice behind me.

"Hey Erin."

It took me a second to recognize him. Out of his blues, but still himself. Ball cap in hand.

"Officer Kessler. Mark. We met yesterday. It's my day off" — his eyes flicked, registering my legs — "and I was nearby, so I thought I'd drop in, see how you're doing."

I kept sweet smiles on standby. "Thanks for thinking of me. I'm, y'know — okay. It's a lot."

"Mmm."

My skirt was too short. I knew it. He knew it. He looked away, up the street, put his cap back on and straightened it.

I had to say something. There was too much silence.

"So … you live around here?"

He sniffed.

"No, up near the university," he said, without looking at me. "Well … just wanted to check in. But I see you're doing fine, so I'll…"

And with that he walked off.

Nothing I could do to make this look good. He'd tell Lomax and Demko, for sure. But that was tomorrow's mess. Today's came first.

It came fast.

May is why they invented air conditioning. Twenty minutes into my walk to Ty's place, the big look-at-my-tits necklace I'd picked was glued to my chest. Ty knew where to find them without any help, so I yanked it off and tossed it in my bag.

By the time I got to Forest Rose, I understood why they call them dirt roads. Dust caked my shins, stuck in dried sweat dots like I'd been dipped in grit. Do real Steve Maddens hurt this bad, or is that the point—pain you can show off?

Halfway there, I found a Dunkin' with a restroom out back, where I washed my legs and stuck my pits under the hand dryer. The place smelled like burnt sugar and fryer grease. My hair was giving strong post-bail energy. I pinned it up best I could and gave the mirror a look.

"That's some bleak shit."

My eyeliner had melted into black rivulets down my cheeks. I wiped it away, drew on a fresh line, drowned myself in deodorant, and set off again. It made little difference. I was still twenty yards away when Ty came out from under Arnie's bay door in his overalls and grinned.

"Jesus, you look like a raccoon."

At ten feet: "Smell like one too."

"Could be worse—I could be a dead raccoon."

"Sure, if you had better hair."

I slumped onto a pile of tires.

"I was at Cedar Ridge, Ty."

I'd never told him where I worked. That was the whole point of Helen: separate lives. He stood in silence, mouth slack.

His face fell. "Jesus… Are you..?"

How do you finish that question? How do you answer? I just put my head down.

He took two steps back, looking off at the horizon. After a moment: "One of the guys here, his best pal has kids there. Did you know anyone who was…"

I still had my head down, but he read it on me.

"Jesus…"

The grief swelled inside me, threatening to

swamp the levees. Any movement, and it could all come tumbling out. He stepped closer—maybe to hug me, maybe to ask—but I couldn't bear either.

Control this now. Cap it. Shove it all back down.

I wiped my nose, sat up straighter. "Christ, I'm thirsty."

He snapped back to here and now, and handed over a cold Coke from the vending machine, already cracked. Ten seconds more silence while I chugged and figured out how much truth he was good for.

"Ty, I need to get to my mom's to borrow cash, but my car is stuck behind police tape at the school. I need to borrow some wheels to get there."

"Can't you just call her?"

"Cops took my phone. They think it has the shooter's DNA on it."

"Shit—you got that close to him?"

"A car, Ty. Do you have one or not?"

"I got twenty on the lot, but I can't just hand them out."

"I just need to borrow one. Two hours, three tops."

He considered. "I guess you can borrow Arnie's. He's off golfing with his buddies. But not one ding—

he loves that car more than his kids."

The look I gave was icier than I wanted. He winced. "Sorry."

I needed this car. *Let it pass.*

"Back by five, or he'll can my ass," he said as he handed me the keys. "And no smoking in it!"

Mom believed in God and Man. I'd heard too much about the first and seen too much of the second to believe in either anymore.

Halfway to her house, I pulled into a deserted turn-off by a patch of woods. In the cramped back-seat of Arnie's BMW, I wrestled out of Helen and into Erin—out of the tight skirt and into the bland, competent suit I saved for job interviews and bank loans. Helen got zipped into a bag on the floor. Never the twain shall meet.

The turn-off gave way to Mom's part of town, where the world went quiet except for the drone of other people's effort: lawnmowers, leaf blowers, the rhythmic *tck-tck-tck* of a sprinkler head watering a perfect bed of azaleas. The air smelled of cut grass, and probably of money too: I wouldn't really know.

She could have come to visit me, of course, but that's not how things worked. The Lord had blessed her with all a sixty-year-old woman could need, except for three things: grandkids she could hug, car insurance she trusted to survive downtown parking, and an immune system that let her anywhere near the kind of folk who worked outdoors. According to her, she'd break out in hives just by driving by somebody picking strawberries.

It's a miracle she got out of the house at all, especially if Pastor Joel DuMont was on TV.

I expected the usual interrogation, the third degree about what I was wearing and why I hadn't called sooner. But the woman who was halfway down the lawn the moment I arrived wasn't the Colleen I knew. She was pale, her eyes red-rimmed, and before I could even kill the engine, she was pulling open the car door. I barely had time to spit out my breathmint cover-story before she was crushing me against her ribcage. For a tiny woman, she's pure Appalachian bear. Years of self-denial, self-improvement, self-righteousness and Pilates. I half expected her to drag me inside for the full ritual mauling. But instead:

"Oh, Erin, honey. Thank God. Thank God you're okay."

She wasn't letting go. I could feel her small body

trembling against mine. It was the most surprising thing that had happened all week.

I had to nearly die before Mom started treating me like I was alive.

She finally pulled back, wiped her eyes, and led me in by the hand like I was thirteen again. She sat me down on the sofa, fussing over me, making tea, acting for all the world like a mother. It was so out of character I didn't know how to react. Even when she said, "You smell like cigarettes," her voice had no hint of accusation.

"It's the cops," I said. "They were smoking. They came by this morning."

Her mouth pinched like a cat's asshole. *There she was.* "They never smoked on duty in my day."

They never did anything in her day.

"What I don't get is why they're bothering you at a time like this," she continued, her old self slowly reasserting control. "You didn't do anything wrong. They should be out looking for him."

"They needed a description, I guess. They're probably asking everyone who... Mom, listen—I need a loan. I'm sorry. I know. But I do."

I expected the lecture, the sigh. Instead, she just nodded, her eyes welling up again. "Of course, baby.

Of course. Anything you need."

Either I'm dying, or she is.

While she went to fetch her purse, I glanced around what she still called the "front parlor." Spotless. Her beloved Queen Anne table, packed with framed photos. And in the corner, the shrine to Dominion of Light. Pamphlets, CDs for the old guard, neatly folded t-shirts with the dove-and-cross logo, each sealed in cellophane to keep the sin out. A pile of on-brand, sky-blue cardboard files—notes, instructions, records—all perfectly stacked.

Except one.

An orange one. Crooked on top of the pile. A cuckoo in the nest.

She came back with her purse wide open, and pressed a pile of twenties into my hand without a word. No guilt trip. No conditions. Just a watery smile. For a second, I felt a pang of something— shame, maybe, for how I always thought of her. Maybe she was softening in her old age.

Then she opened her mouth.

"I suppose he was Black. Don't look at me like that, I know what's on the news."

"Hannity isn't news."

"Even if he wasn't Black, he was definitely an

immigrant."

"Remind me of your ancestry, *Colleen.*"

"That's different. Your grandfather didn't turn up here uninvited with a whole other religion."

"Sure. The Indians were too busy at Mass to fight when the Irish arrived. Tell me, was grandpa from the Shawnee O'Briens, or the Comanche O'Briens?"

She snapped her purse shut. I snapped my mouth shut. The fragile truce was over.

She walked me to the door, all business now. As we got to the car, she appraised me once more, holding me at arm's length without letting go. My entire life in a single gesture. "You look better than usual, anyway. Is that a new car? A BMW. Fancy."

"No, I just borrowed it." Then, because it seemed safer: "From a colleague."

"A teacher?" she said, her eyes narrowing slightly. "Teachers must do a lot better than para-whatevers."

"Paraprofessionals," I said, with a smile that didn't reach anything.

"Well," she said, finally letting me go. "You take care of yourself, Erin. And call me. Don't make me worry like that again."

I picked up a cheap phone at Walmart—five hundred less than I'd told Colleen it would be, so I pocketed the rest, except for two bucks I spent on a cardboard pine tree to hang from the rearview—an attempt to bury the smell of cigarettes under the industrial sting of fake forest, manufactured in Shenzhen and probably illegal in Canada. I didn't have time to put my Helen armor on again before speeding back to Ty's lot. I'd cut it close. As I swept in, his face at the bay door flipped from *having-a-stroke* to *my-job-is-safe*, then confusion at what the hell I was wearing. He'd never seen me like this before.

"Goddamn, H, you look like you're selling Bibles door-to-door."

"Church clothes," I said. "Every day is church day for my mother."

"You take after your dad, then?"

Yeah, but I got my pursed lips from Mom. I handed him the keys in silence. He didn't even notice—too busy circling the Beemer, checking for joyride damage. As he passed in front of me, I leaned into his broad back and wrapped my arms around him, squeezing tight.

"What's this?"

"I'm thanking you."

"I should let you steal Arnie's stuff more often."

"I've been lifting cash from his register for years."

I let him go and we drifted awkwardly apart, with a small wave just as I turned to go.

The pine smell outlasted my antiperspirant, but even that quietly died halfway home. I dropped in at the bank to sink half the remaining cash I'd taken from Mom into my overdrawn account. The slip still showed a negative balance, enough to scare me off looking too hard. But at least I was no longer bumping along the bottom—just drowning without my feet on anything solid. Apparently that was an improvement.

At Kroger on Sheridan Drive I stopped just long enough to grab a six-pack and a frozen pizza. Juli at the checkout stepped back—I smelled like I'd been commuting by dumpster. Who cares? I hadn't eaten since yesterday, I was dirty, I was thirsty, and my stomach was pressed tight to my backbone. At least something in me was holding firm.

Until I turned my key in the door.

Something…

I looked back. Slow. Intentional.

There, across the street, by the vacant lot. A man, leaning against a white four-door sedan. He was older, maybe fifties, early sixties, haggard. Pale skin, dark hair shot through with gray.

Most people flinch when they get caught watching.

He didn't.

He wore cheap sunglasses and a red shirt, a faded hoodie that looked a size too big for him. And as I stood there, key in the lock, he raised his phone like it was nothing.

That's when my backbone gave out.

Click.

I slammed the door and locked everything—deadbolt, chain, latch—hands shaking like withdrawal. My hallway, for the second day in a row, became the spillway for all I'd been holding back.

Baby's Breath

Chapter 4: The Dismissal

"9-1-1, what is your emergency?"

I should have them on goddamn speed-dial.

The dispatcher's voice was a drone a million miles away. She asked how I knew it was the school shooter, and I screamed at her, "*'Cause I was in the fucking school, bitch!*"

Felt bad about that later. Even I wouldn't have believed myself. I sounded crazy. Hell, maybe I *was* crazy, right then. Even so, she calmly told me to find somewhere safe and that a patrol car would be with me in five minutes.

This time I crawled under my bed and waited, cursing myself for being such a Rachel Maddow, pussy-ass liberal. I should have had a gun, like every other motherfucker in the Midwest. When five minutes was finally up half an hour later, and I heard the siren, I was screaming "he's here, he's here," while they were still two blocks away.

But he wasn't. Of course he wasn't.

A female patrol officer took notes while her partner—some goober-looking rookie, all elbows and Adam's apple—wandered the road shining his flashlight under bushes and into car grills, like the killer might be crouching in the mulch.

The guy in the red shirt was nowhere to be found, and other than it being an older man near a white sedan, I couldn't tell them a damn thing. But they took a statement anyway, each trying to out-bored the other while pretending they believed me.

"You say he was the shooter?" she asked.

"Who else would it be?"

"And you recognized him?"

"No, he had a scarf on his face."

She looked at her notes. "Wait, you didn't tell us he was wearing a scarf."

"He wasn't."

"You just said he was."

"At the *school*. Not today."

"So you didn't see his face at the school?"

"Right."

"Then how do you know it was the same guy today?"

There was a pause, just long enough for me to

hear how dumb it all sounded.

"Look, I just *know*, okay. He was here watching me. *Right there!*" I pointed at nothing. "He had a red shirt on!"

Real smooth, Callahan. Next time, maybe accuse a dog or a stop sign. Even the goober could tell it was time for an intervention.

"Ma'am," he explained, in the gentle, patient tone you use on toddlers and crazy people, "lots of people wear red."

By the time they left, I didn't know if I'd reported a threat or pitched a pilot. The adrenaline drained away, leaving me hollow and humiliated. It was pushing eight, I was wired, wrecked, and I still hadn't even started the one thing I set out to do today.

I was alone with the buzzing silence of my own dancing nerves. What now? Crawl back under the bed? Hell, no. The last solid thing I had in my life right now was my job, and I could feel it turning to sand in my hands. At least two local cops thought I was crazy, and who knew what Kessler was already whispering to the school board? I had to get ahead of it. I had to call Principal Greevy.

I prepped. Standing in the kitchen, inhaling like a yoga teacher, exhaling like a liar. Rehearsing the aura of someone professional, someone you'd keep on the payroll. Then I shotgunned a beer, cracked another so it'd be ready, and made the call.

"Hello?" She sounded exhausted.

"Principal Greevy?"

"Yes."

"It's Erin. Erin Callahan, from Lightning Bugs."

"Erin? Oh, honey. Oh, honey." Her relief was a physical thing, a wave of warmth that crashed down the line, and I felt the first hairline cracks appear in the dam I'd built. "How are you? You're not hurt?"

"I'm fine."

"You're okay?"

No. I think I'm losing my mind. "Yeah, I'm just trying to get things together, you know. But—but someone is watching me. Just now, at home. Outside. I just called the cops. I think it's him, I think it's the shooter."

My voice was too loud, too fast. She paused, just a breath. But it was enough.

"That sounds terrifying, Erin," she said, suddenly all Principal. "Are the police with you now?"

Actual worry would've been bad, but this measured concern about my mental state was even worse. I felt the waters rise.

"Erin?"

"Yeah." I was checking the window for demons.

"Erin, are police there now?"

"No, they just went. They just left me here."

"Well, it's probably nothing to worry about then. We're all on edge. Everyone's still trying to process."

Oh, so get with the program, Erin? Della's blood on my clothes is just part of school life now?

Hold it together. Focus. Get what you need.

I stood and paced in the kitchen.

"I didn't know who else to call," I said. "You're the only person who—" I stopped. Recalibrated. "I just... I need to know where I stand."

"It's important to give yourself grace right now."

Grace? I needed a paycheck. This wasn't a friend talking anymore. This was a manager handling a liability.

"I know," I said, slowing my breathing, pressing my free hand to the cool kitchen counter. "I just... I need to know where I stand. With the school."

The pause was softer but heavier, like she'd

dropped a velvet-wrapped brick on my life. "Well, we're still in crisis mode, Erin. There's so much happening. Right now, the most important thing is for you to focus on yourself. The district has grief counselors, support services… We want to make sure you have everything you need to heal. Take some time. Don't even think about work."

"Some time?"

"Yes. As much as you need."

"But what about my job? I still have a mortgage to pay. I need to know if I'm still employed."

Was it the phone line, or did this bitch just click her tongue at me?

"I understand," she said, but any human understanding had been filed away under *This Could Be Expensive*. "But right now, there are a lot of discussions happening. With the board, with human resources, with our insurers. We all need some time. So do you."

"Some time?"

"Yes."

"What? So you're firing me?"

"I didn't say that."

"So what did you say?"

"I mean, you need to look after yourself after a shock like this. Let me worry about the school."

"And I'm not part of the school now?"

"I didn't say that."

That's twice you didn't say that. So what are *you saying?*

"So I am suspended?"

"Let me be clear. The situation is complicated and—"

"Why can't you just answer the question? It's yes or no."

"I understand you're under a lot of stress."

"Complicated for who?"

"For everybody. You're not alone in this."

"Look—" My hand gripped the edge of the kitchen counter so hard my knuckles went white. "Just answer the question, for God's sake."

Greevy never lost her temper. She knew exactly where it was. Slow and deliberate now.

"Okay, I'll answer. You're not under any formal suspension at this time."

"At this time?"

"That's correct."

I waited. Nothing.

The one who talks first loses. Trump said that, and for once, I believed him.

"Am I being held responsible for this?"

"Let me be clear," she said. "The school isn't even open, Erin. There is no work for anyone right now. We strongly encourage you to take this time for your own recovery. We'll be in touch as soon as we have a clearer path forward."

"But I was there," I said, quieter now. "I was in the building. I got blood on me."

A long, slow recalibration.

"Erin, you're clearly under a lot of stress. I think maybe we should continue this another time."

Click.

Chapter 5: The Remembrance

They called it a Remembrance, but it felt more like a public autopsy. The air over Cedar Ridge Elementary was thick with the thudding of helicopters, a mechanical heartbeat drowning the human one.

I'd found whatever somber clothes I could, and walked from East 6th, taking the route I'd walked every school day and then, as I came closer to the crowds, taking the only path available, joining the silent, crushing press of ten thousand bodies.

This was the math of tragedy. Four hundred kids meant eight hundred parents, maybe thirty-two hundred grandparents, and a whole concentric circle of aunts, uncles, friends, and neighbors, spreading out through the town. Some came because they felt it was a duty. Some out of respect.

But for many, it was clear, this was an event to be seen at. The national media had descended like locusts, their white broadcast vans parked with military precision, their long-lens cameras sweeping over the crowd like the turrets of tanks. They were here to harvest our grief.

Rich pickings. The air was heavy, humid, charged with the wet shuffle of an army of the heartbroken, delivering a sea of flowers that spilled over lawn and over the low wall onto Mill Hollow Road—bouquets by the thousand, single roses, dandelions clutched in a toddler's fist—piled around a mountain of soft toys whose glassy eyes stared out with a terrifying lack of comprehension.

My plan was simple: get in, lay a flower, and get out before I fell apart.

The crowd was hauntingly silent, a collective holding of breath. The only movement came from the extremes of age. A few preschoolers, too young to grasp the scale of the horror, darted between legs, their giggles a shocking punctuation in the stillness, their horrified mothers trying to catch them and get them in line. Barely a year older, but a lifetime away, first-graders stood frozen, their faces pale, clutching their mothers' jeans, their thumbs and wrists jammed into their mouths, their eyes fixed on the new, permanent lesson they had learned.

The families of the victims were a separate island, an archipelago of pure agony. They were kept apart from the rest of us by a wall of gently-officious grief counselors in identical blue polo shirts, their logos promising some kind of professional compassion.

They shepherded the sobbing, chest-heaving parents along the edge of the floral sea, pointing out cards, whispering condolences, their hands hovering over shoulders, never quite touching unless a body began to buckle. I watched a man I knew to be Steve Dublin's partner collapse into the arms of two counselors, his howl swallowed by the sheer mass of silence.

I turned away from it—from pain too real, too raw—and that's when I saw her. Mom.

She stood near a makeshift stage, under a portable lighting rig, right beside Pastor Joel DuMont from the Dominion of Light. They'd brought their own broadcast van, its satellite dish aimed at heaven. DuMont's face was a mask of profound, televised sorrow. "This community is strong," he was saying, his voice resonating through the enormous speakers. "We are a family. And in the face of this darkness, we must hold fast to the light…"

And there was Mom, his loyal soldier. In one hand, she held a donation tin. In the other, an iPad, collecting email addresses for the Church. Grief for the families, data for God.

I was a fool to have come here tonight. This wasn't for me. I'd thought I could hold the hands of the parents, the ones I'd handed children to for two hundred afternoons a year. But I couldn't get close, and if I did? They had no feelings to spare for me.

And I didn't want to ask for any. Those kids? I knew them all. I could grieve—I would grieve—alone and forever, without seeing all of this. This was turning into a performance, and I didn't know my lines. I started to back away, trying to slip out the way I came in, whispering my thanks to those who moved to let me pass.

"Excuse me."

The voice was calm, but I flinched anyway. He was right beside me, a man in his forties, and no part of this crowd—a crisp shirt, clean khakis. He looked more like a conference facilitator than a mourner. He wasn't holding flowers, and like me he was moving against the tide.

"Just a terrible day," he said. "I hope you didn't lose anybody?"

"I have to go," I said, turning away.

He took a half-step, just enough to stay in my path. It was subtle, but it was a block. "Are you part of the school? I only ask because you seem to know your way around. Are you faculty, maybe?"

I looked past him, at the blue polo shirts of the counselors. Could I make it over there? "I'm sorry, I really can't—"

"I understand. It's a lot to process," he said, his voice a low, insistent hum. "The little ones, in Lightning Bugs, they were so young."

The world stopped.

The helicopters, the crowd, Pastor Joel's voice—it all receded. A roaring pressure built behind my eyes, the sound of a dam straining against a flood.

Lightning Bugs. He said *Lightning Bugs.*

I looked right at him for the first time. His face was unremarkable, his expression one of mild, detached concern. But his eyes were sharp, focused. On me.

"How do you know that?" My voice was a choked whisper.

"Know what?" he asked, all innocence.

I took a full step back and stared at him, my mind was racing. *Who is this man?* This wasn't mourner small talk. This was something closer, more insidious, right inside my brain, right inside my life. Was this the man who had stood outside my house in the red shirt? He didn't look the same, exactly, but they felt connected. Two men who knew too much. Two men who were too calm in this situation.

"I have to go," I said again, my voice shaking. I started to push past him, faster through the throng now, no longer making my apologies.

"Come back, I just wanted to talk."

I didn't answer, didn't look back, I just pushed hard into the throng.

The fear was flooding in, cold and absolute. This man, this stranger—was he stalking me? Was I safer here, in public? Or safer running from him? I stopped again, looked around to see he'd paused. When he saw me look back, he surged towards me again. I turned left, behind a group of taller men, then ducked, weaving a path, hoping to shake him off. I don't know who he was, but he was part of *it*—whatever *it* was. He had to be. It was all a web, and I was at the center of it, and this man was one of the spiders.

"You are Erin Callahan, aren't you?" I heard him shout.

How the fuck does he know that?

I broke into a run. Fell. Stood again, not looking back, pushing through the bodies until I'd shaken him off, until the crowd peeled away like skin, and I was sure I could make it back home. Safe. Unseen. Alive.

Chapter 6: The Shaming

"Miss Callahan?"

Della, tugging at my skirt.

"Miss Calley? I'm scared."

Bang. Bang. Bang.

The banging now was all inside my head. Pounding, like fists inside a coffin.

Hangovers used to be almost fun. I got to wear sunglasses indoors and have McDonald's for breakfast, ice-cold Coke and salty fries to bring my soul back to life. The nausea would vanish by ten a.m., and by the time the working day was ending I was ready to face another few Jacks with whoever was around from the staff room.

But now?

Kill me, if this is what your mid-thirties are like.

The light was vertical and mean. My sheets had trapped me like a hostage, bound me, and tried to sweat me straight as a punishment. When I finally wrestled free of blankets, I lay there cooling off, face half in the pillow, mouth rinsing itself with that thin, sour warning shot before a vomit.

Helen had it easier. She'd just elbow the guy beside her and mumble, "Make coffee."

I scraped together the parts of me not nailed to the bed, shuffled into the kitchen, and did three solid minutes of groaning, while the TV mumbled in the background. I forgot to turn it off last night.

Do the math. One mug. Two spoonfuls of instant. Three Advil. Four sugars. And then three steps back so I didn't hurl. After a doubtful, wet-mouthed moment over the sink, I zombie shuffled my way to the sofa, and there I was, full-screen on Channel 9.

Twice, in fact. On the left was me, taken from across the street by the vacant lot. I was leaving my home in a too-short-skirt and my come-and-get-it-pumps, Kessler watching me like I'd just stepped off his browser history. On the right was me heading home in bank-loan clothes, a six pack and a plastic bag containing the remains of Helen.

A news ticker below.

TEACHER 'PARTYING' HOURS
AFTER CEDAR RIDGE SHOOTING.
ERIN CALLAHAN, 33, FACING

QUESTIONS.

What. The. Fuck.

I turned up the volume as they went back to the talking heads. They had a panel discussion with a shrink who looked like she was explaining physics to a cat as she said the words *dissociative episode* and *disordered attachment*, and two aggressively blond pit bulls who were having none of this science shit. The network paid them to foam on cue, and they were earning a bonus over me.

"Let's be clear," one of the pit bulls barked, leaning so far forward she almost fell out of her studio chair. "This isn't about trauma. Our sources on the ground tell us this is a woman with a history of *highly* questionable behavior. A woman who seemed more concerned with her own story than with the tragedy of those little ones."

The little ones.

The phrase hit me like a physical blow, cold and sharp. The man at the Remembrance. The one with the clean khakis and too many questions. *"The little ones, in Lightning Bugs, they were so young,"* he'd said, in that smooth, laminated voice.

Our sources on the ground.

My blood ran cold. He wasn't just a mourner. He

wasn't just a creep. He was their source. He was the spider who had been patiently tracing my web, whispering what he found into the ear of a producer. The bastard wasn't just "putting things together." He was constructing my coffin, live on national television.

I put the balls of my thumbs in my eyes and died inside for a few moments. When I came back to life, the pit bulls were reporting "*your* views", which were really just *their* views, bounced back to them on social media.

By the time I finished installing Insta and Twitter on my new phone, it was already too late. #Erin-Callahan was trending. Not in a "girl-survives-hell" way. In a "can-you-believe-this-bitch" way.

> **@TrashCatRising**
> When you'd love to stay and
> save kids during a massacre, but
> you're too thirsty for beer and
> dick.
> #ErinCallahan
> #TeacherOfTheYear

> **@NiceWhiteMom77**
> Say what you want about #Erin-
> Callahan, but… no, that's it. Say
> what you want.

And they did, in more than a thousand replies. Every hateful word was another fissure in the earth, and I could feel the pressure building. It was all backing up behind my eyes, ready to burst.

I stopped reading and uninstalled both apps.

It wasn't even good beer.

Jesus. I really drank all six, didn't I? Then hauled my sorry ass back to Kroger for more. No hat, no sunglasses, no damn sense. I should be grateful nobody caught me staggering home with that second six-pack. But even if they did, it could hardly be worse—hell, I'd already handed the world its headline.

People get cancelled for tweets. I was being cancelled for reality. For being seen. For being who I am.

No call from the cops. Not yet. But they knew. Of course they knew. Kessler had front-row seats. And Demko? Oh, he'd have logged it in that special little notebook of his and probably gifted me his second eyebrow raise of the week.

I could see Lomax now, holding me to the light like a specimen, reclassifying me. I wasn't just a witness anymore. I was a red flag.

How did I not see this coming? How could I be this goddamn *stupid*?

They don't need flashbulbs and news vans any-more. Every pissed-off neighbor with a phone can detonate the worst time of your life across the inter-net in thirty seconds. Then the news picks it up, and boom—your face is on Fox with the Scrolling Ticker of Blame, and you're just waiting for the first death threat.

And I *saw* him. The guy, the shooter, the jour-nalist, the pissed-off neighbor, whoever the hell he was. Leaning against his white car in that red shirt, watching me. I *saw* him. But I was too busy being paranoid to notice that they actually *were* out to get me.

No. No, that's not right. They weren't out to get me at all. I was just a fuck-up.

I dropped to the kitchen floor again. This time, it wasn't to prepare for the shit train rolling towards me. There is no preparing for a train that heavy.

I dropped because I couldn't stand any more.

I was still crying on the floor when my mom called, exactly one minute after her alarm went off at ten. God and dad's divorce settlement wanted her to have plenty of beauty sleep, but I bet she earned a dozen fresh wrinkles when she saw the news.

I let it ring half a minute. Then I picked up, because I knew she'd just keep going until the rapture.

"Do you have any idea what you've done?"

Straight to the meat. That was Colleen.

"Mom, I—"

"Don't you dare say it's not your fault. You think the whole world's blind? You think God doesn't see?"

I really didn't give a good solid shit about God's opinion, or Colleen O'Brien's either. My gut twisted because I was scared she might be right about what the whole world saw.

"Mom, I wasn't thinking—"

"You *were* thinking. Thinking with your pants off. That's how you were thinking. You think I don't know you, Erin Callahan? And now look."

A deadly pause.

"All I want to do is bring Him back into your life, Erin. And you keep shutting the door."

Him with a capital H. That's how tight they were—Colleen and Jesus, sharing a Google Calendar.

"I'm sorry, Mom."

"You don't need *my* forgiveness. If you want forgiveness, go to confession."

"Do they even *do* confession at the—what is it—Church of the Perpetual Offering Plate?"

"You're going to give me your tongue? At a time like this?"

Absolutely arctic.

"We might be in Ohio, but we're still proud of where we're from. I'm still Sean O'Brien's daughter. And we don't forget the sacraments."

She was from Toledo, and Baptist, my ass. That's how Catholics talk. Catholics who hide their hearts in velvet boxes and call it the old faith.

I tried sobbing a little louder, just so she'd cut me a break.

"Stop feeling sorry for yourself, Erin Callahan. Some things need to be cleaned up properly. Or is the Church going to have to step in *again*?"

"Jesus, Mom, that's cold—even for you!"

But she'd already hung up.

I puked twice after Mom, then a third time just for

the taste of it. Nothing much came up except foam and bile and guilt. I put my pounding forehead on the bathroom tile, waiting for the floor to absorb me. From down there I could see a dust bunny behind the toilet base. I let it live.

I saw the envelope as I passed the front door, but I needed a cold Coke first, then circled back. No postage stamp, just the school logo. Delivered by hand. Greevy must have wanted it here fast.

Inside:

> **Pending formal investigation into the events of May 17th, you are hereby placed on administrative leave.**
>
> **This leave is unpaid.**

No *Erin honey* this time. Just "Dear Miss Callahan." It's like they were already rehearsing my disappearance.

I folded it once, then again, then again, until I couldn't fold it anymore. It was the best way to destroy it without tearing. Ripping things up was too childish, even now.

The gas bill was on the mat too. Past due. Again.

A dry, splintered laugh came out like a bark, and shocked even me. Then I went to the back door. Half the garden was weeds, the other half was things I'd once intended to plant. I watched a bee slowly audit the area and change its mind.

I sank onto the concrete step, Coke warming in one hand, cigarette burning down in the other. The neighbors didn't even like me enough to watch me at my lowest point. Half a dozen had a perfect view from their rear windows, but no one twitched a blind as I sobbed until I choked. Not because I'd been suspended. Not because I'd become a meme. Not because of the kids.

Not even because of Della.

Because I knew—knew—I had done this to myself.

Chapter 7: The Canteen

I'd ordered the Uber to pick me up on Cherry Street. No way was I walking out my front door onto East 6th Avenue again. Not dressed like this. Not when every phone within ten blocks was doubling as a goddamn confessional booth.

I'd spent the day grinding my feelings against one another—fear, hate, anger, regret—until they turned to powder, too fine to separate anymore. Now I needed to feel something else.

It had been a long time coming. Eighteen years since Mom, bloodhounding her way up every wrong trail she could find, had driven Dad away with her crusade.

He'd done nothing wrong, except having an old copy of *Barely Legal* stuffed in a box under the garage workbench, and a pretty, dangerous fifteen-year-old daughter in rural Ohio.

Two plus two: five. Top work, Colleen.

Once my changing body started drawing the wrong kind of attention, Mom did her math, and decided dad must be to blame. So he needed to be put away from me. Purged. Banished. Jailed.

And he was.

Nobody asked me for a statement. I was a minor. But Mom? She was a sister of the church and pronounced from On High. Always did. Once she locked in on a sin, it nearly always stuck.

So we stayed locked in too—just the three of us: Erin, Colleen, and Guilt. A messed-up house-share full of secrets, black mold and curdled milk.

God's truth: the man never laid a hand on me.

And when it had all played out—those tight, airless months—and the sin was gone from my life, unacknowledged, unspoken, erased, all I had left inside me was a gap the size of a begging bowl. In a classroom in Lancaster, I'd found twenty-seven ways to fill it. Tiny, perfect pieces. Healing my wounds by hugging other people's kids every morning.

But that wasn't forever. Sometimes school was out, or budget cuts took away the Teachers' Aides. Then the brittle scaffolding cracked, and I fell back hard on another way to fill the void. Men I can hardly remember. Men I longed to forget. Too many beds. Too little judgement. Eddie with the line between his brows, and his blooded knuckles. Married Ty, laying down betrayal as if it was part of the foreplay.

None of this could come near school, though. Are you kidding me? No way.

So I made Helen.

Erin remained clean, kept herself above the waterline, her job safe from the currents that threatened to drown her. Helen handled the overflow, the dark waters where judgment usually swept people under.

But now the job's gone. Not a layoff, not a furlough while the district waits on the debt ceiling. *Gone* gone. Gone for good.

And those perfect pieces are now in tiny, white caskets, leaving me with nothing to do but knock a deliberate breach in my defenses, let the flood in, and drown my sorrows.

Those fuckers can swim.

Screw it. Erin was broken. Erin was a victim, a suspect, a mess. Erin stayed home and cried.

But Helen…

Helen went out. Helen didn't feel shame; she used it. She put on the crop tops and the red lips and walked into the world like a weapon. It was a cold, familiar feeling, the click of armor locking into place around a hollow core. Helen's all I've got left. That's what she's for. An overflow channel, releasing the pressure, letting the waters run for a while without collapsing the whole damned structure.

I took the $250 in cash I'd stolen from Mom and then hidden from my overdraft, and I shoved it into my best purse, along with a half bottle of Jack and a joint for the journey. Over the sagging back fence, through the Garcia yard, onto Cherry and the waiting Uber, and down to Granville Pike.

The Canteen was trying a little too hard not to be a bar.

Low amber bulbs in steel cages hung like mood lighting at a prison wedding. Exposed brick, battered booths, shelves of tatty books bought by the yard. It smelled of wet wool, and the concrete was artfully cracked, like there was some remodeling guy near campus who made his living turning bars authentically miserable. If you stood still too long, your shoes stuck to the ground and you risked walking away barefoot.

Huddles of students nodding along to the music: some sad-sack Englishman moaning about a town he couldn't figure out how to leave. Others at small tables, battering laptops like they were defusing bombs. Two middle-aged professors playing pool in resolute silence.

Nothing could make me be here. But Helen prowled in places like this. Tight jeans, dark eyes, distraction over dignity. And ready to play in the snow. Tasha, if she knew you, could sometimes get you a bump. Officially, signs said you'd be reported and barred, but unofficially, nobody came in the john to lecture you about wellness.

Which is good, because I wasn't in any mood for wellness.

I'd been going at it pretty good while the place was still quiet in the early evening—Blue Raspberry Mad Dogs, one after the other, and half an eye on the door in case Tasha showed.

Not much had gone right this week, so when Eddie walked in with two buddies—each of them shrink-wrapped into their shirts like they wanted you to guess how much their gym membership cost—I barely blinked, just muttered, "Sure, of course," and went back to my drink.

He didn't spot me at first. I'd found a booth near the back, where I could check the whole room for likely targets—thirties would be good, unquestioning, drunk enough, somebody I could forget about tomorrow. And for now, Eddie was too busy calling out the pool guys, raising the volume by twenty percent, drawing the kind of looks that said *you don't belong here.*

It wasn't until the place started to fill that he saw me.

He said something to his boys, and then they all looked over at once. Subtle.

I saw him crack a joke, then square up and step forward to perform his victory dance over the shattered woman at the back of the room.

"Helen Calley," he said, his voice thick with glee. "Or is it Erin Callahan? I can never remember."

I didn't make eye contact.

He sat in front of me, blocking my view of the bar door.

"How do you think you looked on the news?"

I know I wasn't fast enough to hide it, 'cause he crossed his arms and leaned forward with a shit-eating grin.

"Let's not do a scene, Eddie."

"Whoa. She doesn't want a scene now. Doesn't want to act anymore. What's wrong, don't you have any more costumes to wear?"

I'll give him this: he has a boxer's instinct for

finding the pain spot and punching till it breaks.

I kept my voice low.

"Go back to your friends."

"Why don't you go back to yours? Got any left?"

Yeah, actually, I do—and one of them just entered. Tasha, halo curls and slouch jacket, gliding sideways through the crowd by the door.

Thank Christ.

"You aren't the worst mistake I ever made, Eddie."

I stood.

"Just the loudest."

The bathroom light buzzed—cheap, flickering off the tile like it was trying to quit mid-shift.

I'd handed Tasha a hundred, and we went to the ladies' room without a word. She knew better than to talk much. We just found a stall, locked it, and she opened her purse.

I found my key.

Bent forward. Inhaled hard.

Dry kindling. Flame. That coiled snake within me unspooled, stretched, and muscled into life again.

Tasha vanished into the night, and I checked my nose and teeth, then stepped out into a whole new Canteen. The music had changed. I could dance to this.

I made it to the bar, stood on the bottom rail, and shouted my order until it arrived. Glancing left along the counter, I spotted a guy with ink on his neck who looked trouble I wanted to follow me home. I pushed towards him, but he turned away as his girl moved into view.

Fine. Dickhead. Your loss, there'd be someone else. I just veered off again, scanning, making eye contact and breaking, waiting for somebody to hold for a meaningful glance, circling for the right target. The crowd around me grew, and the sound throbbed through the ground, up into me. The rhythm was different to my heartbeat, and I couldn't get things to line up. It got hot, loud, overwhelming. There was no space here. I was suddenly aware of eyes, phones, cameras.

What on earth are you doing? I hissed at myself. *You're still in Lancaster. This isn't witness protection.*

I needed air. Darker, cooler corners of the bar called to me, but the spaces felt too exposed, the crowds too dangerous, and going out to the parking lot meant passing Eddie and his two stooges by the door.

I turned towards the back of the room again, away from the bar, where it was still quieter—a shelf with seats and sports posters screwed to bare brick. Most of the stools were free, just a couple chatting and a guy alone with a book and a laptop, some hipster in a thrift store sports coat, testing out facial hair, maybe a PhD student, maybe the last lecturer to call it a night.

I kept my back to the room. If nobody could see me, nobody could photograph me. I just had to stay here until it was gone—either the powder-jitters or the entire internet.

The guy in the corduroy coat next to me glanced up from his book.

I must've looked half crazy, stood there, too high to sit down, too paranoid to walk into a crowd. I was just facing the wall, beside an empty stool, like it had kicked me out.

He looked puzzled for a second, then decided I wasn't his problem and turned back to reading.

And for some reason, that set me off, looking for a fight.

"What's your story, moustache?"

He looked up again and glanced around to check I didn't mean some other moustache.

"Me? Oh. I am a man who will fight for your honor," he said, with the same flat tone as a guy telling you he fixed vending machines.

I opened my mouth, then closed it. I didn't know how to fight with that.

He tucked a finger in his page and leaned in like he had a secret. "I'll be the hero that you're dreaming of." Then he nodded and went back to his book.

Okay, so he was a prick. A smarmy, book-reading prick. That, I could work with. I'd find another way to get under his skin.

"Boy, did you choose the wrong bar to be clever in."

"Starting to think that," he said, eyes on his book.

"Maybe the wrong state."

"I'll take it under advisement."

He'd completely derailed me. The fight I'd been itching for had evaporated, replaced by... what? Annoyance? Curiosity? I couldn't pin it down. But the rage had fizzled out. I could face the room now.

I walked away, then looped right back.

"Oh, we're still doing this?" he asked, looking up again.

"I like your moustache."

"You do?"

"What are you, like, a Civil War reenactor?"

And then I reached out and poked it.

What in God's name are you doing Erin? You're poking his face.

"It's my power center."

"So if I shaved that off…?"

"I go limp, like a fish."

"Hey, that happens to a lot of guys sometimes."

He nodded over my shoulder, into the crowd.

"I bow to your wide experience in that area."

What the hell did that mean? Jerk. What a jerk thing to say.

I turned on my heel, not sure if I was gonna cry or punch somebody and walked smack into Eddie, who'd seen me talking to this dweeb and decided to come back for Round Two.

"Do you lie to everyone Helen, or am I special?"

"No," I said. "You're not special at all."

I was rolling now. Forget this guy.

"Should have known," he said, breath hot with beer, "should have known all that teacher crap was pure bullshit. Well? Wasn't it?"

"Hey," I said, smiling like a blade. "I got mine."

He put his bottle down and stood close. Spoke close.

"You think you're fucking smart?"

"Why—do you think you're fucking stupid? 'Cause that'd be the smartest thing you ever figured out on your own."

Not my best idea. His brow knit. Eyes white. Face red.

Then—

"Wow," said a voice just to my left, soft and dry, talking to itself. "Advanced peacocking in downtown Lancaster."

Eddie's head jerked sideways.

"What the fuck did you say, college boy?"

After it was all over, we sat on the low wall under the bar sign.

"You should keep your mouth shut in future."

"Didn't think he'd hear me."

"What do you think now?"

"I think I'll keep my mouth shut in future."

"You know," I told him, "it takes a certain kind of man to carry off a moustache."

"Yeah?"

"And you're not one of them."

"You think I should shave it off?"

"No, no, no. I think you should *laser* it off. If you just shave it, there's a risk it'll grow back."

The corner of his mouth twitched. I liked that—his tiny responses. I dabbed at his nose again, then poked him with another question.

"Doesn't the hair feel stiff when you get blood in it?"

"Oddly enough, that isn't a situation I've had to navigate much. Not until I met you, anyway."

He squinted at the torn paper in my hand.

"Wait, are you wiping my nose with *Lincoln in the Bardo*?"

"I'm drunk," I said. "I'm not basic."

But yeah. I was.

I told him I'd pay for his Uber. He said he didn't

need one—he lived just around the corner.

"Sorry about the book. And your nose."

"The nose'll heal," he said, touching it gingerly. "The book, though? My boss is going to kill me. I borrowed it."

"I'll hide the evidence," I said, shoved the useless remains of the book in my bag, and held out my hand.

"Erin."

"Noah."

He turned left, away from the baying chaos of The Canteen.

I turned right.

Chapter 8: The Names

Names were released to the public the next day.

I saw it on the TV, locked in my home with the curtains pulled tight against any more press. I couldn't stand the sound being on. I couldn't even bear to look at the screen. It all felt unreal, like a bad soap opera, like something beamed from another galaxy.

This can't be true. Not these names. Not people I know.

TV was where they made things up. I needed confirmation.

By midday I'd pulled myself together enough to call Ray Garcia, even though I could've walked to the end of the backyard and shouted over the fence. We'd exchanged numbers last year, so he wouldn't have to bang on my door at two a.m. This was the first time I'd used it.

"Mr. Garcia, I need a favor. Could you grab me a copy of today's *Eagle-Gazette*? I'll give you the money, I just—"

I'm not sure who's gunning for me more: the shooter, the media, or the families.

"—I just can't leave the house right now."

He caught my tone. Whatever he thought about his dumbass neighbor all over the internet, he was still decent, clockwork-steady Ray Garcia. Fifteen minutes later, he passed the folded paper over the fence and waved off my money.

I took it inside and hugged it like a lifeline.

Holding it made it real. Not pixels. Not headlines. Just names. On paper. In print.

I folded it twice, tucked it in the drawer, and sat. I didn't read it again. I didn't need to.

The pain was overwhelming.

Eight dead from my class.

Javier Cruz. Mikayla Jennings. Braden Keller— sweet Braden, who couldn't even tie his laces. Aaliyah Thompson. Connor McIntyre. Sofia Gutierrez. Lashka Patel, whose parents had already lost a child in a car crash and started again in their forties.

And Della Morrison. Della, with her weird obsession with octopus. Her odd, skipping run when she saw a dog outside the fence. That knack she had of deciding to grab my hand and hold it at the exact moment I was balancing twenty-seven sets of coloring pens. That morning, she'd come to me beaming that her mom had sewn new pockets into her skirt, pulling the bright orange linings out—wild against the bottle green—and showing them to every child in the class. Della. Gone.

And four more in the hospital, one critical. Emily Rourke. She was already scared of loud noises.

Was? Is. C'mon, Erin. She could live. She still could.

A sharp rap on the front door sent a jolt of pure adrenaline through me. A killer wouldn't knock, but a journalist might. I crept to the peephole, my stomach a slipknot tightening with every step.

I saw the uniform first and felt a wave of relief.

Then I saw the face.

Kessler.

"Sorry to bother you at home, ma'am. I heard about the call—the one you made about the fella across the street. I wanted to apologize for—" he cracked half a smile, self-deprecating, knowing "—well, for those two idiots who attended your call yesterday. These younger kids… you can't teach experience, know what I mean?"

I felt a small, stupid flicker of relief, and undid the chain to open the door fully. "It's okay."

"No, ma'am, it's not. The last thing you need is to feel like you're not being heard."

The last thing I need is anyone paying attention to anything I do or say.

Has he not seen the internet?

He offered another small, reassuring smile. "I'm gonna give you my direct cell number. You see anything, you feel anything, you call me, okay? Day or night. You understand?"

He handed me another one of his cards. I already had one. This time it had his cell phone number handwritten on the back.

"Thank you… that's really kind."

He paused, his eyes doing a slow scan of my face. His tone shifted, losing its formal edge.

He put one foot over my threshold, into my house.

"Listen, Erin… I also heard there was some trouble at The Canteen a couple nights ago. A report of an assault."

The relief I'd felt curdled instantly. "I don't

know… I didn't see anything. I don't think I did."

"That's not what I heard," he said, his voice dropping lower. He took a half-step closer. Was this still a welfare check? "I heard you were there. That you were seen helping some college kid with a bloody nose."

The man was fifty, if a day, and was protecting and serving.

What the hell is this?

"Hey, we all need to blow off steam, I get it. Especially after what you've been through. But that kid you were with…? Kid like that can't take care of himself, never mind take care of you." He watched his hand run up the doorframe. "You should find somebody who can look after you."

He was standing close enough to smell him now.

Why would a beat cop wear cologne?

My hand tightened on the doorknob, but he just kept smiling, like he knew a secret I didn't. "Call me," he said. "Call me if you need anything. You got my number."

Oh, I've got your number, all right.

The levee was holding. But the cracks were spreading.

Tasks. I needed tasks.

I wiped my face and sat up. What could I do? The place was as spotless as I could make it without paint cans and a new kitchen. My drawers and cupboards were now forensically clean, and I didn't have lessons to prepare for, or crayon drawings to label. I needed something—anything—that I could do with my body instead of my mind. I'd tried my usual route the other night, and didn't need that again. I needed a function. An errand. A purpose.

I needed funeral clothes.

That could work. I liked that idea. It could mean a whole day of not thinking. That would work.

The school might be dicks, but they'd surely let me know when the services were being held. I knew every parent—I'd handed their children back at the end of a hundred days and more. I should be there for them. I should be there for the kids this time. Couldn't let them down again. I had to show that much respect.

I'd taken $250 cash to The Canteen, and now I had $122. What a goddamn idiot. But even with what was left, I could get a cheap suit in River Valley

Mall, couldn't I? Maybe spend a hundred?

Damn, I needed my car. When was the school gonna open so I could retrieve it—even if just to sell it? Until then, it was more money on Ubers.

I swung a leg over the fence and dropped onto Cherry Street, slipping a five in Ray Garcia's letter-box as I cut through his yard.

I had black shoes already. I was sure I could find two pairs of tights with runs in that I could combine into one—I'd seen some during the Great Clean-Up. A black jacket and shirt in Ross Dress for Less cost me just sixty, which was the first piece of even mildly good news I'd had in days. It meant I had a spare few dollars, enough to pay for my Uber to make one extra stop on the way to my last destination of the day: Johns Memorial Library.

I stopped to check my reflection on the glass before I went inside.

The doors hushed behind me, leaving me looking at a world of low bookshelves and open-plan echoes. Somewhere near the back, a printer kicked into life, and it was enough to raise complaining heads from those at study between the rows of books. Even the silence here had a way of drawing attention.

"Hi," I said too loudly to the woman at the counter, all flyaway hair and cardigans.

"How can I help you?" she whispered back.

It took me a moment to describe him to her, but a couple of minutes later, Noah came walking across the floor towards me wearing an apron, with a small pile of old books in his arms and a question mark written all over his face. I've never seen anybody look more completely at home—and more utterly perplexed.

We stood close, speaking in secret little voices like naughty children.

"Hi again. Nice to see you, but what are you doing here?"

"I brought your book back."

I reached in my bag and pulled out a fresh copy.

I'd stuck a pom-pom bow on the front.

His face cracked wide.

"Well, thank you—that's really kind. Thing is… I actually bought a copy this morning."

He pointed with his chin, and there it was—top of his stack.

Ah, crap.

"It's okay, you keep it. You read it."

"I just… I wanted to do something nice for you. I feel bad about Eddie."

"Eddie? Oh. Eddie. Right. We weren't formally introduced." He tilted his head, suddenly curious.

"Wait—how did you know I worked here?"

I hauled the carcass of his old copy out of my bag, and held the front inside cover up to his face. Stamped inside:

Johns Memorial Library
Ohio University Lancaster

"Plus, you said your boss would kill you. Two and two."

"Shit. You should work for the police."

"Yeah, it's a bit more complicated than that."

He gave me a look—somewhere between amused and concerned.

Not the moment to explain.

I shrugged.

"Well, I already have the book," he said, and coughed. "Sooo… I guess you still owe me."

"Guess I do."

"So… erm…"

He hadn't done this in a while.

Maybe never.

"How about you give me your number?"

I stopped.

"It's okay—no pressure."

"No, no. It's not that, I want to, it's just… this is a kind of a crazy time."

He looked like he'd heard brush-offs before.

But I owed him more than that.

"Gimme your phone."

He laid his pile of books very carefully on a table, like setting down a sleeping baby, and reached into a back pocket.

I typed my number in and dialed myself, smiling.

"You don't spend much time on Twitter, do you Noah?"

Chapter 9: The Interrogation

I made my way back across the Garcia garden, and in through my back door. For the first time in days, the world had stopped spinning like a sickly fairground ride. It felt calmer now. I had my feet down.

I made coffee and tried reading this goddam book. Paragraph after paragraph of God knows what—like a homework assignment. Footnotes, for Christ's sake. I half-expected a pop quiz at the end. Googled four times before I even hit page three.

Noah wouldn't mind if I dropped it, would he?

I mean, he might not even call.

Screw it. I grazed my way through *Marie Claire*, and it wasn't until near two that I finally spotted the business card waiting on my front doormat.

Detective Gabriella Lomax
Major Crimes Division

On the back, a hand-written note asking me to

come into the station on West Main for some follow-up questions.

Oh, the fun never ends.

I flung on fresh jeans and called the Uber guy back to Cherry Street, giving Ray a little wince— *sorry*—as I passed his door again.

The Fairfield County Sheriff's Office was as low and flat as oatmeal. Maybe the architect had a thing for linoleum and drudgery, because it carried on inside, steeped in the municipal smell of floor cleaner and two-gallon tins of budget coffee.

The guy behind the glass took my name without looking up, buzzed someone and pointed me to sticky plastic seats bolted to the floor. I flumped and checked the news on my phone.

I was off the front page at least. Maybe I was already yesterday's villain. Maybe I'd get lucky, and some poor bastard would reverse a minivan into a cheer squad. Better yet if he's an immigrant. I could be off the hook entirely by Monday.

After fifteen minutes a young cop came to fetch me. Down a corridor, up a yellowing stairwell, and there at the top stood Lomax, already holding open a door.

The wooden sign across it said Interview Room Four.

"Can we get you a drink, Erin?"

"Thanks, I'm fine."

Lomax and Demko sat opposite me—she: stark and clean, her navy jacket slung over the chair so I could see her arms. A feather tattoo peeked from under her rolled sleeve, just the curve of it, inked close to the bone. Leather notebook, closed, and a pen.

He had even less: no frills, not even an expression. Just a stack of index cards, like his own personal game of solitaire, each one turned face down.

Lomax started it.

"Thanks for coming in, Erin. We've been gathering as much as we can about the background to the shooting, and we just need your help filling in a few blanks. Just so we're clear, this conversation is being recorded. That okay?"

"Sure."

She pointed to the corner of the room behind her head. A small black dome on the ceiling. "Audio and video, right there."

"Okay."

"Ready?"

"Ready."

"Okay, let's start. Erin, do you know a man called Edward Francis McLure?"

Immediately off-balance. My heart gave a single, hard thump against my ribs.

"Yes."

She left a long, pregnant pause, letting it cook, letting me wonder.

Why are they asking about Eddie?

"How do you know Mr. McLure?"

"He's—well, he was—a friend."

"A boyfriend?"

"Um, yes."

"And how long were you in a relationship with Mr. McLure?"

"We weren't in a relationship, it was more like a—"

Normal people finish sentences for you. Cops don't. Their job is to make sure you finish the whole of every sentence.

"Eddie was just a hookup sort of thing. For maybe six months, off and on."

She nodded, and looked at Demko.

He flipped over his first card, his movements

crisp, economical. He placed it carefully beside the stack on the table. I could see his neat handwriting on it, but not what it said. His turn to speak. He sat bolt upright as she leaned forward on her elbows to watch me.

"Was he ever violent?"

"No. With me? No."

"With anyone."

"I mean—Eddie is Eddie, know what I mean?"

She said, "No. Why don't you tell us what you mean."

"Well… I've seen him in fights. In bars."

"So he has a temper." It wasn't a question.

I shrugged.

"You have to say it, for the record."

"I guess. But he never hit me."

"Did he hit a man in The Canteen Bar on Granville Pike two nights ago?"

My stomach clenched into a cold, hard knot. *Kessler.*

I could only manage one word: "Yes."

"Why were you meeting with Mr. McLure on Wednesday?"

"We weren't, he was there with his buddies."

She studied my face. "Do you know his buddies?"

"No". *I never met their friends. Separate worlds.*

"And who were you with?"

"Nobody."

"Drinking alone? On a Wednesday night?"

I tried a small, brittle smile. "It's been a tough week, y'know."

She nodded. He watched. He tapped the desk—once, a sound like a gavel.

"Did you meet Eddie on the seventeenth?"

I froze.

"That was the day of the shooting at Cedar Ridge Elementary."

"You think I don't remember that?" My voice was sharp.

He shrugged, unmoved. "You seem to have forgotten a lot of things that day."

"Like what?"

"Like Edward McLure was seen parked up outside your home around midnight."

"I—whoever told you that… I don't know anything about Eddie that night."

He waited while she wrote something down.

"I mean—I don't know about him *earlier* that night. What he did. He came to visit, just to see if I was okay."

They both sat silent, looking at me, as my words ate one another in the dead air. She made a second note.

I could hear my own breathing.

"Back to the bar," said Demko, his voice flat. "You were seen leaving with an unknown man."

"Just into the parking lot, and then I went home. Alone."

"Who was the man?"

"He said his name was Noah."

"Had you met him before?"

I shook my head.

"Do you know how we can contact this Noah?"

"No."

Why the hell did I lie? Shit. That was so stupid.

Lomax turned slightly to Demko. He gave a tiny, almost imperceptible nod. She turned back to me, her expression unchanged.

"We arrested Mr. McLure last night. Felonious Assault."

"That's up to eight years," he added.

They let the silence stretch. I managed to close my mouth.

"Would you be surprised to learn Eddie has an unlicensed firearm?"

"*Jesus*, Eddie!"

"So you are surprised?"

They didn't expect an answer this time. The weight just sat in the room.

"Okay, let's leave that there for now." Lomax stood, went to a water cooler in the corner, and returned with two plastic cups. She slid one across to me.

I finished mine in single gulp. She sipped hers. He seemed not to need one, like a lizard.

"Have you ever met a man called Darnell Mathis?"

"Darnell? Sure."

"And how do you know him?"

"He's the school janitor. Is he okay?"

"So as facilities manager, he'd be in charge of—what? Maintenance, fixing stuff, that kind of thing?"

"I guess."

"And that would include the school security cameras?"

The air left my lungs.

"I—you'd have to ask Principal Greevy."

"I'm asking you."

"Could I get some more water?"

"In a moment. Would Mr. Mathis be in charge of the CCTV on school premises?"

"You tell me."

I knew they'd tell me. I even knew what they'd say.

"We didn't find any footage of the shooting."

Just do it. Drop the goddamn hammer.

"When we questioned Darnell Mathis, he said you told him to turn off the cameras."

"Why would you do that, Erin?" she asked, plaintive and concerned.

I stared at my hands, trembling in my lap.

"Because I was buying weed and didn't want to be seen."

"From Darnell?"

Just shoot me.

"Yes."

My voice had shrunk so small now that it vanished into the silence.

"So the reason we don't have any picture of the suspect—?"

"Is me."

We took a break. At least Lomax did. She stood and twisted her shoulders. Demko appeared to be a robot, absolutely impassive, just sitting watching me. I'd asked for water, so she brought it, another plastic cup that I downed in one.

She threw my old cup into a waste basket with practiced ease.

The hardest hour of my life was just another Friday for her. Each question she asked, each knowing glance they exchanged, felt like a crowbar against the stone. I could feel the emotions, a churning river, pressing hard against the barriers I'd built, threatening to spill over.

He flipped another card face-up, and we were back into it.

"You're not a qualified teacher, are you Erin?"

I just shook my head. I wasn't ready for more yet.

But they had no intention of letting me rest.

"I need you to answer for the tape, Erin."

"No, I'm not a qualified teacher."

"So you work as a paraprofessional?"

"Yes."

"And in that capacity, is it normal for you to be alone in the classroom?"

"I mean—sometimes, for a few minutes."

"But usually, you're not trusted to be alone."

"Hold on, what do you mean, *not trusted*?"

"I mean a teacher needs to be with you."

Absolutely unflappable.

"Yes, usually."

"So why were you alone when the shooter came into your class?"

I shook my head. Took me a moment to recall—

"Oh. Right. The air conditioning unit was dripping."

"So the teacher"—she checked her notes—"Fran Loxton went to see Darnell?"

"Yeah."

"Why didn't she send you?"

"With Darnell? You gotta—let's just say he doesn't jump for just anyone."

"So what you're telling me is that the senior, qualified teacher left the unqualified paraprofessional alone with the kids, just so she could go nag the janitor."

These weren't questions. They were accusations, polished and laid out like evidence.

"And that meant you were all alone, the exact moment the shooter arrived."

Miss Callahan?

I wasn't saying anything now.

Miss Callie?

"Just you and him."

I'm scared.

"Do you know who the shooter is, Erin?" she said.

"No, I don't."

"You're sure you don't know anything else about him? Anything we should know?"

"Yes. No. I'm sure."

Blood thumped in my ears. We all sat silent as

statues.

Then, like she'd touched a button, he popped back into life, flipped over his next card and laid it on the table.

Straight back to the same old pace. Relentless. Each question accompanied by a hole you could fall into.

"Do you remember the first day we came to your home, Erin?"

"Sure."

"You said then that you hit the shooter with your phone. Do you remember saying that?"

I nodded.

She pointed to the ceiling.

"Out loud, for the recording."

"Yes, I remember." My voice was too loud, too defensive.

Calm down.

"So we took your phone into evidence."

"Yeah, I remember that too. Can I get that back yet?"

She looked at me, wondering. Something about this slowed her certainty. Still—job to do.

"Unfortunately not. In cases like this, Erin, we work with the FBI. They have a lot of forensic expertise."

"Okay."

I felt shattered. Wasn't listening.

"And they did a forensic examination of the phone in a real hurry."

"Active case," he said.

"Inside and out," she said.

Right. Wait, what the hell does that mean?

"Extraction and analysis."

"I don't know what that is."

He looked to Lomax, as if he didn't do explanations in person.

"We have experts who go through the device," she said, "looking for clues. Emails, messages, web history, geolocation, that kind of thing."

"Okay."

I had no idea where this was headed, but they did. She took what felt like half a minute examining my face, looking at her notes, considering. Whole time, he didn't take his eyes off me. I don't think he blinked until she eventually glanced at him.

And then he took over.

"Who is Helen Calley?"

Shit.

"Who?"

"Don't be dumb, Erin, this isn't the time. Helen Calley. hcalley236@gmail.com."

I sat very still.

"Why is that email account on your phone?"

I knew my mouth had twitched. No way he didn't see it. I looked from one to the other.

What the hell is happening here.

"Do I need a lawyer?"

They both leaned back, satisfied. A shared look. The game had just changed. No pauses now. They'd done this a thousand times. It ran like a play.

Her: "I can't really answer that, Erin".

Him: "Probably not, if you've got nothing to hide from us."

Her: "You can have one if you want one, though."

Him: "Give me the name of your lawyer. I'll get the front desk to call him now."

Beat. And cue Erin.

"I—I don't know his name."

Whose fucking name? He doesn't even exist, you crazy

bitch!

"Well, give me the name of his company, and we'll look him up," he said.

"If you don't know a lawyer," she said—it was like watching tennis—"you can get a court-appointed one."

"But"—he looked at his watch and inhaled through his teeth—*sheesh, what a shame*— "it's just after five on a Friday. You'll have to wait in holding until one gets here on Monday morning."

Oh, you clever bastards. You timed this perfectly.

"Or we can press on," she said.

I closed my eyes.

"What did you want to know?"

"Who is Helen Calley?"

"It's me."

They didn't flinch. Of course not. That trap was already set.

"It's odd to use an assumed name, isn't it, Erin?"

"I use it for—for Tinder. It's hard enough holding down a job as a paraprofessional, without—"

Without being known as the town slut.

"So this is just for dating?" she asked.

I nodded.

"Is that the name you and Eddie used?"

"Yes."

"Do you know what *conspiracy* is, Erin?"

I looked at him, for the first time genuinely scared.

"Do you know what *conspiracy* is?"

"I think so."

"The FBI did forensics on the flowers too."

I felt a cold dread.

"They're from Bloom Room," he said.

"Where's Bloom Room, Erin?" she asked.

"It's on my street."

"Do you know what geolocation is?"

I nodded. My mouth was ash.

"The FBI did geolocation of your phone. On the sixteenth—that's one day before the shooting at Cedar Ridge—you took a call from Edward McLure while you were right outside the Bloom Room."

I remembered it. He wanted to come over and screw. I told him I was tired. I wasn't even in Bloom Room—just grabbing smokes at Kroger next door.

"I—"

"Want to know whose DNA was on those flowers?"

I'd learned now how this worked. Whatever he was gonna tell me, it had already made my gut freeze over.

He counted them on his fingers.

"Yours. The shop assistant's. And nobody else."

She leaned in and read from her notes: "*'After a crime what happens if I don't answer questions?'* Why did you Google that twelve hours after the shooting?"

Ohmygod *ohmygod OHMYGOD.*

"I was—it was just after I got home from hospital. I was trashed, I couldn't remember what happened and was worried I'd…"

Fail questioning? Well thank God you Googled how to avoid that.

He pivoted again, keeping me constantly off-balance.

"Did you know Eddie had an unlicensed firearm?"

"No, I didn't fucking know, okay!"

A long breath.

He flipped his next card, his next trap.

She said, "Do you need a break, Erin?"

What good would it do?

"No."

She nodded, sat back. Read half a page of her notes and began again.

"We understand that your father is estranged from you?"

What the hell is this?

"You could say that."

"She did say that," he said, cold as a blade.

Lomax shifted. Looked uncomfortable.

But he was leading now.

"How long since you saw him?"

"Pfff. Forever."

"You haven't seen him recently?"

"Not since I was a kid. Fifteen."

"You got an address for him?"

"Nope. My mom might. Colleen O'Brien."

"We know who your mom is. And he hasn't visited recently?"

"Like I said, I haven't seen him for—I don't even know what it is. Eighteen years?"

"He has a police record." She put a finger on a

line in her book. "Unlawful Sexual Conduct with a Minor."

"Yeah, and talk about being railroaded."

"He was convicted."

"I know that!" I snapped, "Jesus, you think I don't know this shit?"

They let the charge fizzle out of the room, and then he continued.

"He was released ten years ago."

"Probably." I felt exhausted. "We lost touch."

"He served eight years and was released. Is that when he moved to West Virginia?"

"I didn't even know he was in West Virginia."

"FBI forensics did an examination of the outside of your phone as well."

"Oh, so we're done with painful family history, and back onto phone hygiene, now?"

He looked at me, amused that I'd even considered fighting back.

"Do you know what they found?"

"That Eddie shot up my classroom?"

The amusement vanished.

"Joke," I said.

"Now's not the time for joking, Erin."

He said, "Do you know what the FBI found?"

"How would I know?"

"They found two traces of DNA on your phone. One is yours. The other is a close familial match."

"To who?"

"To you."

I had no idea what he was talking about. She was still sitting back, arms folded, considering.

"What that means, Erin," she said slowly, "is that some near relative of yours has come into contact with your phone."

Wait, what—?

"Could your mom have touched your phone recently?"

"No. I mean… what are we talking? Days, months?"

"Less than four weeks."

"I don't know, but I don't think so."

He turned over the last card. They were all on the table now, daring me to bet against his hand.

"Was your father ever violent?"

"Absolutely not. He's a good guy."

"A good child abuser."

"That's not right. They didn't even let me give evidence."

"And you haven't been in contact with him since?"

"How many times? No."

"And do you know it's a felony to lie to the FBI?"

I could feel a hammering in my neck, hear the flood of my own pulse.

"I haven't lied to the FBI."

"Have you lied to us?"

Think quick, Erin. What have I actually said in this room?

"No."

The lie tasted like metal in my mouth. Noah works at the library.

Shit.

"And you're an only child?"

"Yes."

Would you want to mate with Colleen twice?

"So it's not your mom," he said.

"And it's not a sibling," she said.

He finally moved, leaning in slowly, his eyes glittering behind his glasses. He smiled, sharp and tight.

"Then tell us, Erin—how the hell did your father's DNA end up on your phone?"

Baby's Breath

Chapter 10: The Flood

I couldn't decide what the cops thought I was—the genius behind a mass-murdering criminal conspiracy, or a coked-up moron they could play with like a terrier with a rat.

Maybe I was both.

Whatever. They didn't charge me or even attempt to hold me. I told them I needed air, and they said I was free to go, so I did. The moment I turned away, the tears broke loose. Then the entire edifice split open, a full-body shudder giving way to a torrent that swept me straight out of the building, through the hot screech of traffic, and directly into a liquor store for cigarettes and Jack Daniel's.

Didn't give a single sanctified shit about open bottle laws. What was one more felony? I popped the lid before I was out of the store, and was a quarter bottle in by the time I made it a block along and found a bench outside the Glass Museum, where I sat and shook and cried and screamed. A woman passing by looked like she might come and comfort me, but was afraid of being bitten.

When the sobs turned to panting, I looked up at the museum. I used to bring kids here on field trips once a year. They were usually bored, and so was I, but I was paid to sound excited, so I made the effort. Truth is, I could never make anything out through that wavy old glass. Was that because it was so old, or had things always been that way? Maybe things in the past were just constantly vague. Maybe I was crazy to expect better today.

I sat and philosophized about this until I realized the marble bench had frozen my ass to stone.

I stood and looked around. The sun was starting to dip, long shadows crawling across the traffic. Another swig, and it hit me: I'd blown my Uber fare on Camels and whiskey, and I was still miles from home with Jell-O for legs.

Cars rushed by like the world had better places to be. I just needed one of them.

Mom was probably the last person I had in the world—and the last person I wanted to see. Couldn't call her.

Ty would be sitting down to dinner with the Holcomb household, and it turns out my genes had blown up enough families for one week.

And Eddie couldn't help me without digging a

tunnel.

I took a swig and scrolled through my contacts—the graveyard where I buried bad decisions. Jesus, who even are half these guys? No time to find out. I had one bar left on my phone.

And the ones I did know? I'd either screwed them or screwed them over, and in most cases: both. Only one name wasn't either. My last incoming call.

I barely knew the guy. Two conversations, a fat lip, and a busted copy of *Lincoln in the Bardo*. But he hadn't ghosted. He hadn't posted. He hadn't even tried to touch me.

And right now, that was all the résumé I needed.

You busy? Need a ride.
Downtown. Glass Museum. x

I hit send, poured the last quarter bottle of Jack Daniel's onto a flowerbed, and waited to see if anyone still gave a damn.

His car was a piece of junk, but when I told him so, he stopped lecturing me about the benefits of mouthwash, and started taking corners sharper.

"What, you sulking now?"

"I'm not sulking."

I murmured he should tell his face that, and cracked the window.

"Thank God," he said. "Fresh air."

"What do they pay librarians anyway?"

"Less than you, I imagine."

I doubted that, but no way I wanted to talk money with him.

He hadn't explained why it took him close to half an hour to get to me. He'd parked as close as he could—not close enough in my opinion, which I also let him know about. But walking over to him gave me time to notice he was wearing a much cleaner jacket and cardigan than last time, and it gave him time to take in the smeared eyeliner and the reek of whiskey. I raised an arm and shouted his name. He offered a smile that tried to pretend his evening hadn't just taken a sharp turn for the worse.

For some reason my seatbelt wouldn't fasten, so he had to do it for me while I focused on finding some better music. He asked where we were going, and I turned up the radio and told him, Alley Park Lake.

I thought about letting him screw me so I could forget about spending my life in jail for just one hour—then I looked at his corduroys and moustache, and figured it'd be three minutes, tops, so barely worth it.

What the hell. We were nearly there now. May as well finish the car crash.

I was already loosening my jeans when we reached the lake, but he didn't even slow down. He swung the car around, and said he'd love a really strong coffee right now—and could he make me one too?

We compromised on him dropping me at my place. We were almost on East 6th when I remembered my doorstep was home to half the Lancaster press and an armed lunatic, and rerouted Noah to Ray Garcia's instead.

Later I'd realize why he wanted to walk me to the door. At the time, I assumed he was just being a gentleman. The process took a while, because I got quite involved with the sagging back fence, and at that point Ray came out to check things were okay, and looked sharply at Noah.

"It's fine, Ray. He's just a friend."

Ray looked relieved.

Noah looked resigned.

"So," said Ray, "we're all okay here?"

"Peachy," I said, and gave him a smile that didn't make it all the way.

He dipped his head to look at my face.

"Maybe you come into mine for a bit, huh? I have the good stuff inside."

"Yaaay."

But it turned out he meant coffee.

His mugs matched the coasters. This must be what a grown-up kitchen looks like. He'd painted the units a smoky blue, and either he or Connie had done something—I couldn't tell you what—with the lighting. It was low and comfortable.

Nobody filled the silence. It filled us.

My eyes itched and I closed them until the room spun. Better open them again.

As I sat up to face the coffee, my foot touched Noah's. Neither of us moved.

"Sorry about your garden," I said to Ray. "For showing up like that."

"You didn't show up. You came home."

He hadn't asked how I take it. It was just a pitiless black. It's fine. Who wants pity?

They chatted, eventually. Not much. Ray asked

Noah where he worked, and they started talking about the smell of books, about shelf systems, about how Ray once tried to cook using a recipe torn out of a 1970s community cookbook and ended up feeding his family something that tasted like turpentine.

Somebody else was doing the work, and it felt beautiful.

At some point Ray woke me. The horizon was holding still now, so we had a second attempt at the fence, Noah climbing over first while I leaned against Ray. Once Noah was in my garden, it seemed reasonable that he should get me inside safely.

We said goodnight to Ray, but he waited on his back step until Noah had poured me a glass of water and backed out.

I heard them a minute later.

"She's had a hard week. Good kid. Treat her right."

"We're just friends Mr. Garcia."

"Name's Ray," he said. "And there's no *just* in friendship."

Baby's Breath

Chapter 11: The Offerings

I point-blank refused to do Saturday morning. Just lay there, mostly face-down, slowly concluding that this—this right here—was why God let the Christians bump the Sabbath to Sunday. No way a benevolent Almighty would let His creation suffer this badly on a holy day.

I had to get coffee. Needed food. What I didn't need—ever again—was another drink. My mouth tasted like one of those fuzzy toilet rugs old people keep around the bowl.

Luckily, I couldn't afford whiskey, which made the decision easier. Or luxuries like vegetables. I'd be eating ketchup pasta until I figured out how to land another job.

I hoped I still had the receipt for the funeral clothes. Maybe I could get a refund. No way I'd be welcome at the services now. Not after trending on Twitter as Little Miss Dick Parade.

My dad, though. *Jesus.*

I didn't think the cops had me down as conspiring with the shooter. Not really. In the room, it had scared the crap out of me. Because how the hell do you prove you've never thought about killing a kid?

Every mom I know has told me they've mulled it over.

Even with a shitty court-appointed lawyer, I could probably handle the search history. Darnell. Lying about Eddie. Even Helen, which was really the excuse for all of them. There was a true story behind each of them—shameful, but true.

But the DNA?

The only way somebody's DNA ends up on my phone is from when I hit the shooter as he came into the room. And that DNA said: my dad.

What. The. Actual?

I lay there and went over it, round and round, getting nowhere. Did Dad send the flowers too? He probably had my address. He definitely had my number. He'd called, what—three Christmases ago? Told me not to mention it to Mom.

I did, 'cause I knew she'd be pissed.

So why did I lie to the cops? Pretend I hadn't heard from him in eighteen years.

Also, Noah's moustache is a disaster.

Nice hands, though.

Bang. Bang. Bang.

Miss Callahan?

Not now!

I'm scared.

Whoever was pounding on my door this time would have to wait until I'd splashed cold water on every part that stank or was sweaty. Which was every inch south of my eyelids.

I trod heavily down to the door and opened it without peeking. Killers don't knock for that long, and anyway, right now he'd be doing me a favor.

Sunlight hit me like a threat as I squinted into his face and whatever he was holding up. Press badge.

Of course.

"Erin."

"Fuck off."

"Erin," like we're on terms. "Erin, don't close the door. You're gonna want to hear this."

I turned back, planting a hand on my hip, the other still gripping the door.

"Am I now?"

That was Colleen's bog-Irish venom, right out of my mouth.

"Two minutes. Nothing you say to me will be reported. No tapes."

He held open his coat like he expected me to pat him down.

"Listen, I'm not here to stick a mic in your face or drag out tears for TikTok. I know what this is like. I've covered five of these things now. Oxford, Parkland, Uvalde…"

I gave him a look. He noticed.

"I'm not local," he said, holding up his press badge again. "I'm national, D.C.-based. Accredited. I get that you're wary—you should be—but we're not ambulance-chasers. We actually vet things. We're diligent."

There was a gap in my armor now. He made right for it.

"Not saying it's the same here as Parkland or the others," he added quickly. "It's never the same. But it's always the same. You know? People rush in, bloggers, fucking—sorry—YouTubers. They're like jackals. Grab a photo, rip it out of context and act like they know you."

I hated how reasonable he sounded. But I hadn't closed the door.

"It's not fair to the families," he said. "Not fair

to people who are just trying to survive."

"Okay. So—what?"

He stepped forward, lowered his voice. This was just between us.

"Look," he said, "You've been through hell. First the shooting, and then... I saw Twitter. Facebook. I thought Fox was disgusting. Always is, but... the way the narrative's been twisted? The tragedy here in town? That's not on you. What I think is important right now is that *you* take hold of the story. Don't let it be shaped by vultures and the internet. You need to make this something on *your* terms. *Your* voice."

He leaned in like he was handing me salvation.

"My network would pay ten thousand for an excl—"

Slam.

I heard him still saying my name though the door, as I rested my head on it. Assholes, all of them. Like he can say *ten grand*, and wipe everything clean. Like money is a healing balm.

It was bullshit. A hustle. All of it.

But I had to admit—he knew the number. Ten grand could keep me afloat. For that I could get a realtor, get to a new town, and try again.

What am I saying? For ten grand he'd make me

infamous *everywhere*. Where was I gonna go that his national D.C. corporate pigs didn't broadcast? How was a make-over and a softball confessional going to make me come out loved on the other side?

If Hillary couldn't manage it, what hope did I have?

No.

For ten?

Not for ten.

I opened the door again.

"Ten grand isn't much."

He rocked on his heel, considering, calculating.

"I'd have to talk to my station manager. But I bet we could get it to twenty."

I wrapped my robe around me tighter.

I didn't even have grocery money, and he's talking about twenty grand. I could feel the heft of it in my palm. The warmth of all those bills.

I knew that kind of dirt would be forever. But even if I couldn't scrub myself clean, maybe I could turn it into something else? Dirty ink into a souvenir tattoo.

He could see me. One more word, and I'd fall.

"Time for a comeback. Like Lazarus."

"A *comeback?*" I spat, and the word sat on my tongue like a trout.

"I'm not fucking dead."

Having made yet another good friend in the media, I once again felt like I couldn't step out of my own door.

Hey, at least I'd be well-trained for prison.

Don't think about that. Don't think about any of it. Just keep moving. Just keep busy.

I finally understood how prey animals felt. The moment I showed weakness to that first reporter, the scent went out. Now they all knew I was in here. Wounded. The bangs against my perimeter started less than five minutes later. It wasn't knocking anymore. It was a hungry, rhythmic thumping that vibrated through the floor. They came in waves— first the front door, then a hammering on the window, then shouts from the side of the house. They were testing for weak spots, hunting for cracks. I yanked the curtains shut, but I could still feel them circling—carnivores who'd forgotten they were ever human, drawn to the soft kill inside.

The only way to my back door was via the Garcia property, but that barely slowed them down. They pulled a van up outside his house and stood on top of it, trying to get a picture of me crying through my kitchen window. When I drew every curtain and blind, they began making brazen forays across Ray's yard and over the fence, hunting for any sliver of glass that might reveal me, balled up tight in my own home. It only stopped when Ray called the cops. At least that kept them away from the rear of the house, and for a moment I thought they'd given up at the front too. They withdrew. The banging stopped. The voices silenced—

And then:

"Lancaster PD", followed by a huge fist on the door.

I crept to the peephole and felt a fresh dread wash over me.

Kessler.

Oh, for the love of God.

I had to let him in. Whatever he had to say, I couldn't have him saying it in front of the nation's hungry press. I pressed flat against the wall as he stepped into the hallway, then slammed the deadbolt home. Locking myself inside with him.

He just stood there in my hallway, a wall of official blue preventing my escape, eyeing my raggedy old robe and hair dragged into a panicky knot.

"What's all this?" he asked, a teasing grin on his lips. He slowly took off his cap and held it over his groin. But I kept a collection of sweet smiles for moments like this, stored right next to my pepper spray.

"Thanks for coming."

He walked into my lounge like it belonged to him. I stayed right where I was, by the exit.

"Well, we had reports from a Mr.—" he took out a small notepad, "A Mr. Garthia". He made the C into a TH, and snapped his book closed with distaste. "He said you're being harassed, and they've been on his property too. But you don't look harassed. Looks to me like you're a girl who knows how to beat men off."

Great. You truly are a master of the single entendre.

"Well, I've told them to stay away from the property. So you should be fine now."

"Fine? I can't go out."

"You need escorting?"

"What?"

"I dunno. Maybe your boyfriend can take you. Where is your boyfriend, anyway? Is that the guy we locked up?"

Are you kidding me right now?

"Are you gonna move them along, or not?"

"It's a free country, we've got a free press. I can stop them banging on your door, but I can't stop them writing the truth about what they see outside. I saw it too."

"I don't know what you're talking about."

"I saw how you looked, couple of days after the shooting. Everyone did. What—you don't have Facebook?"

I felt my face redden. He'd come here to keep the intrusion outside, but he'd dragged it right into my living room.

"Doesn't matter to me," he said, moving towards where I was standing by the door. "I thought you looked good enough to eat."

"I'm—I'm fine now, officer. Thank you for your time."

"Any time."

I stood close to the wall, out of sight of cameras, and opened the door.

"I mean, any time," he said, screwed on his cap, and left.

Chapter 16: The Loaner

So I showered, 'cause wouldn't you? I felt him in the air, on the doorknob, on the carpet. Changed the bedding. Two loads of laundry. Even put away the dry stuff from last week.

I was just starting to panic that I'd run out of ways to keep my mind off my mind when there was a tiny tap at the back window.

"Leave me alone," I shouted.

"Bruff cffee," he said.

I opened the door, took one of the cups, and waited as he removed the book from his mouth. "Brought coffee."

"Oh my God, yes. Where were you at ten this morning?"

He stepped inside and looked around. "So you're a girl who cleans when she's hungover, huh?"

"I'm wired wrong on the inside."

I took off the lid and sipped. Scalding hot.

"Sweet Jesus, that's good. Thank you. I'll kill you last."

Noah smiled with his hands in his pockets.

"Is that for me too?"

"Oh, right." He'd dropped it on the counter when he came in, a slim paperback. *We Are Animals.*

"This one's about a messed-up family. I thought of you."

"I'll treasure it."

"Uh-huh," he said. Not buying a word.

I'm usually good at this kind of thing. But we just stood there, sipping coffee, while he looked around for inspiration.

"I just saw Ray," he said, thumbing over his shoulder.

"Thank you for yesterday, Noah. Thank you."

Was I gushing? Get over it.

"Any time," he said.

I beckoned him through, and dropped onto the sofa. He took the stiff seat by the yellow dresser.

"Except Wednesday mornings," he added. "I have a staff meeting. So no breakdowns on Wednesdays."

"I must have been…"

He beamed. "Kind of a handful. Ray said you'd had a hard week?"

I sat back. I think he really had no idea. I could have lied—probably should have—but instead, I took a deep breath, and began to explain.

The coffee was gone before I was halfway through, and although he listened the entire time— didn't fidget, didn't interrupt to tell me what *he, the man* thought about it all—he stood suddenly just as I got to the part about murdering Black-Eyed Susans with Jack Daniel's outside the Glass Museum.

"Jesus Christ, was this chair a gift from someone who hates you?"

He moved over and sat beside me on the sofa.

Ty would've held my hand. Eddie would've pondered out loud if a blowjob would cheer me up.

Noah just sat there—personably, solid—until I was ready to go on. And I was just about to when there was a soft knock at the door.

"I gotta fix that doorbell," I said, with a sorry smile, as I tried to work on a response to this asshole journalist that wouldn't make me sound like a shrieking banshee in front of Noah.

It was Lomax. Pantsuit intact, but her cop stare gone. She looked tired.

"Oh, great. I was hoping you'd come back to ruin some more of my life."

"Erin, can I come in? I need to talk to you."

I moved aside and she saw I wasn't alone. He'd stood up as she entered, and now stepped forward with his hand out.

"Noah," he said.

"Gabi Lomax."

She turned to look at me.

I gave her teeth. Yeah. *That* Noah.

"No Detective Demko today? What—did he get trapped in his vespiary?"

She didn't bite. Didn't even blink.

"He's at a scene," she said, "but I just needed to drop in before I head over."

"Okay. You're here. What do you want?"

"Listen, Erin. I'm here to say, I know you're probably not going outside much, but just… just be careful."

I was starting to feel bad for goading her. She seemed off. Shaky.

"Why?"

She hesitated, her eyes flicking to Noah and back to me. "You tell me if you see anything. You call right away. 9-1-1, me, or Alex Demko.

I stared at her. "Tell me what happened."

She looked at the floor. Then at Noah.

"Someone tried to kill Tyler Holcomb."

Baby's Breath

Chapter 12: The Break

He'd been fixing a fender in a noisy workshop—power tools, WCOL blaring—when a hole appeared in the panel next to him. He didn't hear a shot.

Apparently, the big dumb ox had been baffled enough to go over and investigate the hole, but when the next one appeared, it finally clicked, and he ran like hell. Lomax said he was terrified. The attending cops couldn't get a lick of sense out of him.

Then Demko—that absolute machine—had remembered the name from my contacts list that the FBI gave them. They'd ignored his record at first. Eddie had been at my home after the shooting, so they assumed he was the only guy I had on a string. Plus, I never phoned Ty, in case his wife found out, so there was no recent history. Nothing that suggested he was anything but the guy who serviced my car.

That's all he'd been, at first.

"None of my business," Lomax said, bringing me back into the room. "I just need to know how it fits." She paused, searching for a way to say this without passing judgment. "I guess if his wife found out... most murders, most attempts? Husbands killing wives. Wives killing husbands. It could be that simple."

I looked at her. What did she want from me? A confession? Absolution?

"Could she have found out? Were you two careful?"

"I think we were."

She shrugged, just a little. "Okay. But if it doesn't fit with the wife..."

"Sorry," Noah interrupted, his voice quiet. "Who is Tyler Holcomb?"

Lomax glanced at me. *Your turn.*

I turned to Noah—just in time to see the question in his eyes curdle into disappointment before I even opened my mouth.

"He's a guy I've been..." I didn't finish.

"I see," he said, the words flat and cool. He looked down at his half-empty coffee cup as if contemplating its depths. He didn't look at me again. He simply turned to Lomax.

"Do you need me for anything?"

"No, sir. I don't think we do."

And with a quiet click of the back door, he was gone.

My knees gave a warning shudder. I sat before they quit, and fixed my eyes at the wall ahead, focused on holding it all in.

"Listen, Erin," Lomax said gently. "I have to get up to Arnie's garage. I can't stay. And I know this is a hell of a moment to do this, but I need to ask you something."

"Right. No, it's fine. I get it. Go ahead."

She didn't sit. Just turned toward the kitchen and spoke without looking.

"Did your father have any reason to want Ty Holcomb dead?"

And there it was. The question I couldn't answer.

Life. It just goes on, doesn't it? Even when you just want it to slam on the brakes to let you cry.

Even when your maybe-boyfriend has just walked out.

Even when your ex-lover is having a breakdown because somebody tried to kill him.

Even when the cops are asking whether your long-gone dad has a motive for murder.

Even when you aren't sure what any of this has to do with you—but the undertow still pulls you under, drowns you, and dumps your body on a rocky shore.

Even then. Life goes on.

The words echoed in the sudden, crushing silence of my house. It came creeping in like fog. I ran a hand over the wall, rough with old paint. I showed Lomax out, then froze in the hallway. But standing now felt like a job. Lomax was gone. Noah was gone. The only thing left was the hum of the refrigerator and the lingering scent of his good coffee, a ghost of a comfort I no longer deserved. The shock had burned through me, leaving behind the kind of terrible, crystalline clarity that only comes with sobriety and despair. I sat on the edge of my sofa, the springs groaning, and for the first time, I let myself see the whole, ugly picture.

And the first thing I saw was that I was an idiot to have trusted any of them.

The cops hadn't protected me. Maybe they never would. The man in the red hoodie who'd been watching my house, the one I'd screamed about to a pair of bored patrol cops, the one who had photographed me from across the street—that was him.

That was Garrett Callahan: my disappearing father, my returning executioner, leaking the photos on the internet, kicking off my moment in the spotlight. He'd left a trail of death through my classroom, then stood outside my home to take a souvenir shot of the fallout. And the police hadn't done a damn thing. He could kill me five minutes from now, and the official report would probably list the cause of death as *"hysterical female, asking for it."*

Okay. Some of that's on me. Seeing seventeen people get blown apart will do that. But I'd made things worse, just by being myself.

Nobody beat me up for that as much as I did.

I was the one who asked Darnell to switch off the cameras at school so I could buy a twenty bag. Then I'd sent Fran Loxton out of the classroom on a dumb-fuck errand because I still owed the guy that twenty. It might've saved her life, but still.

And I'd probably wasted days of Lomax's time chasing Eddie, when I could've just told them he's a punchy moron with a good body and the organizational skills of a drunk toddler. The guy couldn't coordinate two shoes, let alone plan a massacre.

Finally, I'd lied about Noah to keep him out of it. Wouldn't stop Demko. I'd just set him up to burn through another useless week making life hell for a local librarian.

And you shall know her by the trail of her dead.

Christ, I'm sorry, Noah.

Truth is, I'd been a difficult witness because I'm a fucking screw-up, and that's the bottom line. But the cops? They were supposed to be professionals. I can't be the first screw-up they'd had to deal with. Why was this so hard? They had the resources, the databases, the cars and the helicopters, the FBI and the lab-coats with their little brushes and cleanliness obsessions. The whole weight of the state behind them—and they were still flailing.

I saw the interrogation room again in my head: Demko's flat, impassive stare; Lomax's careful consideration. It was an act. They weren't looking for the truth; they were looking for a story that fit, a narrative they could close. They had taken every broken piece of my life—every shitty decision, every grubby secret, every desperate compromise—and built a cage around me. My nights as Helen, my score from Darnell, my affair with Ty, and that idiot fuck-boy with his stolen gun. They weren't just facts anymore. They were bars. They'd twisted everything until the innocent parts looked guilty and the guilty parts looked monstrous.

And Kessler. Jesus. He wasn't a mistake or a bad

apple; he was just the rot you found when you looked close enough at the barrel. These guys are trained to smell weakness and wield authority. Is it any wonder they end up as predators in a uniform? Him, those two goobers who'd dismissed me, the tech at the hospital—if that was law enforcement, I'd take my chances alone, thanks.

My grief had been a storm inside me, a wild, roaring sea I could barely contain inside the dam I had built. Now it froze solid. I'd decided: I wasn't going to just sit here and wait for him to come back. This wasn't a slasher flick, and I wasn't some stupid girl cowering under the bed for the crazy guy to come back with an axe.

Fuck that.

If my father was the monster, I was going to be the one to find him.

Baby's Breath

Chapter 13: The Stonewall

But how?

I paced the worn patch of carpet in my living room and audited my assets. No car, no leads, and barely any money. Great. The cops had his DNA and all the transport they wanted. But they also had to battle bureaucracy and warrants. And for every Demko, they had ten Kesslers. My dad could be in Mexico by the time they got their act together. The only advantage I had, the only connection I could exploit, was family.

And that meant Colleen.

My stomach clenched at the thought. A visit to Mom's wasn't a conversation. It was a siege—and I had no ammunition. But she kept records of everything, especially grudges. If anyone knew where Garrett Callahan had crawled out from, it would be her. It was the only move I had. Convince her, and I find the start of his trail.

I checked my purse again. Seventy-three dollars and change. Enough for an Uber there, and if

I was lucky, enough for the ride back. It was an all-or-nothing gamble, my entire net worth wagered on the hope that my mother might, for once, choose me over her instinct for clean, bloodless punishments.

The following morning's Uber was a ten-year-old Chevy Cruze that smelled enough of stale cigarettes to fend off my growing longing, and enough of coconut air freshener to make me want to commit a murder. I sank into the cracked vinyl of the back seat and watched my weary neighborhood slide by, until fifteen minutes later, we reached the other world—the one where Mom held court. The air here didn't smell of anything at all. It was scrubbed clean.

When she answered the doorbell, she somehow managed to combine, "I didn't think you'd show your face around here so soon," with a look of genuine pleasure.

She summoned me inside. No parlor this time. Perhaps the Dominion of Light enclave in the corner couldn't stand another unsanctioned visit from this heathen.

In the kitchen she watched her coffee machine slowly do its thing with sinful pride—which lasted until I skipped the pleasantries and said, "I need to know where Dad is."

"Why on earth would you ask me that?" she said, recoiling. "After everything he did."

"He didn't do anything," I said, the words a reflex.

Except kill seventeen people, stalk and terrify me, and botch a hit job on a serially unfaithful car mechanic.

"I won't have you bringing that man's name— that man's trouble..." Her hand fluttered to her chest like I'd served a formal notice of plague. "Erin, I won't have you bringing that man back into this family!"

"I need it Mom. It's important."

"Haven't we had enough embarrassment recently?" she asked, with a pointed look at me.

"Embarrassment? Jesus, Mom, is that what matters most?"

"We have to live in this town, Erin. So yes, as a matter of fact, it matters."

She shoved the coffee in front of me. If a saucer could be angry...

"Erin, I know all this—violence—has been hard on you," she said.

You worked that out all by yourself, did you?

"But you can't use this as an excuse to make things even worse. You've got to pull yourself together. You can't afford to lose another year."

"Well, whose fault was that?"

"I hope you're not suggesting it was mine?"

Aaand there she is—all flint and fables.

She blinked, and reset her voice to *pious* again. "I'm trying to bring Him back into your life."

"Doesn't He have better things to do?"

"Well, I could say the same about you. You're a thirty-three year old woman, you don't have a college degree, you're destroying your reputation all over the television. And now you're turning your back on—"

"Jesus, Mom! I don't want God. I want a *life*."

"You think you'll get a life with that man?"

That landed a little too precisely. Was that just a coincidence? Does she know he's connected to all this?

Should I tell her?

No. She'd just shut down. Too much social stigma.

"Mom, I won't bring him anywhere near here. I've heard he's in West Virginia somewhere. I just want to visit him. Out of state." *What would pluck at her heartstrings?* "I've been thinking about mortality since the shooting."

That didn't move her one bit.

"And about forgiveness."

Okay, that hit a target. She looked at me with a strange sense of recognition, as if she'd was prepared to accept that deep down, I was just like her after all.

"Well," she said. *Here it comes.* "I have no idea where he is. I haven't spoken to that man in eighteen years. And I never will."

She stared at me, her face now unreadable. Was it simply spite? Or was this her twisted idea of motherly protection—keeping me away from the man she'd convinced the world was a monster?

"Okay, fine. But you must have something—a piece of paper, a receipt, a name. Just enough to get me started. If you don't know where he is, at least give me the name of his parole officer, or his lawyer."

She barked a laugh—sharp, short, cruel. "His lawyer? Oh, so you'll believe his lawyer now? The man you called a shyster because he arranged the plea deal? You wouldn't listen to him then, but now? Oh, now he's Mister Trustworthy?"

She had me there. I pushed away the coffee,

untouched, and she walked me to the door. As I stepped over the threshold I turned back—if she couldn't help one way, maybe she could another.

"Mom, I can't get my car out of the school lot yet, and these Ubers are costing a fortune. I just... I need some help. A loan. Just until I can—"

"Of course," said Colleen with an iron smile. "Just pay me back the money you had to go out partying." And suddenly her worst Sunday Best was back. "The whole world saw it. God forgives. But you make your choices, Erin, and you live with them."

"Unbelievable," I whispered, half in awe of her capacity for calculated malice. The door clicked shut, sealing her pristine world off from mine. The lead ahead was cold. The bridge behind was cinders. And I was stranded as the water rose.

I walked until I was out of her neighborhood and back in reality, then sank onto a low brick wall outside a closed-down laundromat. My hands wouldn't stay still. I fumbled in my purse hoping for a stray cigarette somewhere amongst the lint and odd pennies. Nothing but a dead vape pen and a broken nail file.

Of course.

Defeated, I pulled out my phone. An Uber was out of the question. That meant three hours on foot—and three hours to imagine all the ways this could go wrong. And it was just after midday in late May: the kind of baking heat that made metal too hot to touch and the air smell faintly of tar. No air-conditioned car to rescue me, no helpful ride. No Eddie. No Ty. No Mom.

No Noah.

What now?

I sat there on the wall, the bricks radiating up through my thighs, the sun flattening everything it touched, and tried to think. The lawyer. Maybe I could find him on my own. I Googled: "Lawyers in Columbus Ohio."

My screen filled with hundreds of results. Page after page of smiling men in expensive suits, their firms named after a string of interchangeable partners and qualification acronyms, rolling across the screen like the chemical formula for financial ruin. After ten pages of unfamiliar names and faces, my hope shriveled and died. He could be dead too, whoever he was. It had been eighteen years. That lawyer was long gone.

What else could I do?

I had Dad's number. It was right there in my contacts, an entry I hadn't looked at in years. *Dad.* But I couldn't just call a killer and ask him to turn himself in. If it was that simple, even Kessler could do it. All I'd be doing is giving him a heads-up that I was looking for him, and put him on my trail.

But maybe... maybe the number itself was the key?

I'd seen it in movies. A reverse phone lookup. Was that a real thing?

I typed it into Google. The first result was a site with a garish, flashing banner:

FIND ANYONE, 100% CONFIDEN-TIAL!

It felt like a scam, but it had that lock icon in the search bar, and a-little-more-than-four-star reviews from a service I'd heard of. Nowhere near perfect, but it was the only option I had left. I copied my father's number from my contacts and pasted it into the search bar. My heart hammered against my ribs as a progress wheel spun.

We found ONE result.

A wave of relief washed over me. For a second, I thought it had actually worked. Then the next line appeared:

Pay $29.95 to view full report.

Shit. Shit, shit, shit. I looked at my Uber app. A ride even halfway home would be thirty-five dollars. I could find my dad, or I could eat for another couple of days. Not both.

I stared at the screen, the blinking cursor a tiny, mocking heartbeat. Find the monster. Or starve while he keeps hunting me down.

"Fuck it," I muttered to the empty street. I dug in my bag, dusted off the cursed and addictive credit card I swore I'd never use again, entered the details, and hit the pay button.

The screen buffered. The little wheel spun. Payment accepted. And then, it delivered the result.

An address.

**182 S. Skidmore Street, Apt 3B,
Columbus, OH 43215**

I remembered it. A walk-up in a dilapidated, multi-unit brick building in Franklinton. He'd rented it for pennies, seventeen years ago, while he was awaiting trial.

I felt my lungs flush out and my heart give up. No way he was still there. No way they'd hold an empty rental for nearly two decades. I'd just pissed away thirty bucks on nothing. I'd have hurled my phone into the passing traffic, but it was the only thing I had left.

I stood up, my legs feeling heavy and useless, and began to walk towards home, half my mind on the problem of avoiding the press, the other half on the problem of avoiding a maniac father with a sniper's rifle.

How else could you track someone on the internet with no money?

There had to be a way. Maybe Google could tell me, or—is The Dark Web a real thing, or did they make that up for dramas? How could I get on there? I could barely use Facebook.

Wait—

Facebook.

It was a crazy, long shot, but old people used Facebook. Even ex-cons, maybe. If he had a profile, it might have a town on it. Even better, what if I could log in *as him*? I wouldn't just get his town; I could get his messages, his friends, maybe his full address.

I stopped, sat cross-legged in the roadside fox-tail, and opened the Facebook app. Logged out of my own account and tapped "Find your account."

I pasted in his number.

The screen blinked. Then a name appeared: Garrett Callahan. My fingers froze. I should've felt relief. Instead, I felt… I don't know. Dirty. Like I'd stepped in something I couldn't wash off.

I hit "Next", then "Forgotten password?"

A new screen loaded.

Send code to g****n@aol.com?

I stared at the asterisks—an email address I couldn't even guess, a seven-letter password to a life I never knew… Screw my last remaining property, I now wanted to hurl my phone into the nearest brick wall.

Instead, I shoved it back into my pocket. A dead end, flanked by its dead-end friends. My last gamble had failed. No lawyer, no login, no money, no ride. Just me, three blistering hours of walking, and the cold certainty that somewhere out there, the monster who'd built this cage for me was still moving. And he was coming back.

Baby's Breath

Chapter 14: The Church

I'd hit the wall.

It wasn't cinematic. I didn't scream or collapse on the floor with a bottle of Pinot, singing *Un-break My Heart* into a wooden spoon. I just stopped. This was a quiet breakdown. The math-doesn't-math kind. The kind where the numbers don't add up and the ideas don't come and your legs are too heavy to pace anymore, so you just sit there, letting the silence press against your ears.

I hadn't given up. I just couldn't see my next move—and even if I could, what kind of move would it be that had to cost... well... nothing?

That was the problem. Finding someone takes money. Not a lot, maybe, if you're smart—but more than I had. You need a bus fare, or a tip for a guy who knows a guy who doesn't ask questions. I've seen this movie. You need to bribe a secretary, or pay for a background check, or buy a shot in a dingy bar for someone willing to talk.

Or maybe just buy a damn charger so your dying

phone doesn't crap out right before the map loads.

Everything cost. And I had nothing.

Even dreaming felt expensive now.

So I stopped. Curled on the sofa. Pushed Noah's impenetrable book aside and re-read two days' worth of old magazines that sold me a lifestyle I had no business dreaming about. I couldn't even spare change for the latest copy of the magazine. I wasn't going to cry. There was no point. I was too broke to afford catharsis.

At some point I was going to have to think of what my next job would be. I seriously doubted it could be with children again—no doubt Greevy would poison the grapevine against me, and even if she didn't, I was plastered all over the news. I just had to hope any prospective employer spent his evenings and weekends in an isolation tank. Frankly, I could have happily sat on my collapsing sofa until the repo men came to take everything away. What was the point of anything more?

And that's when the doorbell rang.

I hadn't invited her. She just materialized—no warning, no text—for the first time in God knows how long. Her eyes swept the room, recently cleaned to within an inch of its life by a crack team from police forensics, and then maintained with desperate precision a cracking daughter with too much time on her hands.

Wasn't enough.

"Well," she said, carefully finding a spot to leave her purse, where she presumably thought it would be safe from the rats, "At least you've got time to keep house again. So that's something."

Let her have her fun.

"I try," I said.

She sat on the sofa, stood slightly, moved, and sat again. A tiny *moue*, and then:

"The problem with this new fashion for big sofas is, they look fine in a properly sized parlor. But they just swallow a room like this."

I took a slow, calm walk to the rear of the kitchen and opened the blinds fully, so God could see what his rep was up to.

"I don't have any good coffee, but I can make you an instant."

"I'll just get one on the way home."

"So you're not planning on staying long? Shame."

She sniffed, unimpressed, and got down to business.

"I know you'll say I'm preaching, Erin, but

I'm here on behalf of the Church. I've come here because, well, we've got a proposal."

Oh. The Church of We, now, is it?

She tucked herself in, neat as an apple-pie. "I spoke to the Pastor *in person* after the service today, and he says the Church is willing to offer you a role. Community outreach in the Youth Ministry. Working with children again. You like that. As far as I can tell, you've been good at it. You'd be doing something meaningful. Something healing."

"For them or for me?" I asked, crashing at the other end of the sofa with a mug of what Folgers calls coffee. "Or healing for you?"

She didn't rise to the bait. She just leaned forward and placed her hand on my knee.

"I want you to do this, Erin. I know you're cynical, but people get saved by God all the time. And if you do it, well, I can give you an advance on your inheritance. Five thousand dollars to get back on your feet, if you take the offer."

I sat up for that. Partly because I could start dreaming again. Partly because I'd just found out network news would pay four times what God was offering.

After she'd left, I sat with it for hours, weighing it like a courtroom jury, proing and conning until the scales gave out. I'd be under Colleen's thumb for the rest of my life—and, if God had His way, all of the eternity that follows. But short-term, five grand would clear a whole bunch of past-due bills.

It also reincarnated a hope I'd just laid to rest. I still didn't know how to track my dad, but I'd stopped even thinking about that, back when I knew for sure there was no way of financing anything more rigorous than a half-assed flip through the Yellow Pages like it was still 1998. But with five grand... It didn't solve the problem of not having leads. But it gave me permission to believe I might find one. At least I could afford to dream again now.

And even if that came to nothing, I'd be working, working with children. Sure, they'd be the children of Baptists who thought Harry Potter was the Devil's way into their homes, but that's not the kids' fault. And it beats scraping burgers at McDonalds on Memorial Drive.

All I had to do was completely forget my ethics, or at least, whatever I'd imagined my ethics were. Who was I kidding? Do people who fuck married mechanics and abandon children get to have ethics? Whatever I'd built my idealized self on, it was falling to pieces now. I needed something more solid if I was going to do this. The waters were lapping at my feet. I needed a hand up that wasn't money or make-believe, but that's all Colleen had in her life. Moral support, that's what I needed. And a bit of forgiveness—the secular kind.

He picked up on the second ring, but didn't speak.

"Noah?" I said. I heard him breathing. "Noah, listen... I'm sorry."

A pause. "Yeah, me too."

"About everything."

"I don't think you're responsible for *everything*."

"Yeah, but what Lomax said—I mean, some of was true. But it's not like it sounded. Me and Ty... it was a mistake, and it ended a long time ago. Months."

"Yeah?"

"Before any of this. Before... before you."

"You don't owe me an explanation."

"I kinda do."

He sighed—not sharp, just tired. "Yeah. I guess you kind of do." A long pause. "But really," he went on, "You mostly owe me a coffee."

That got me. "So... are we still friends?"

"You're such an idiot."

I hopped up onto the kitchen counter and swung

my legs. Felt as if I was breathing again.

"What, why am I an idiot?"

"We're already friends," he said. "I mean... you've seen my apron."

"What—is that like, a sacred rite?"

"It's basically third base."

"Then you've been doing it wrong."

"That apron's erotic in ways a woman like you wouldn't understand."

"It has cartoon olives on it!"

"They're limes," he said, deeply serious. "With faces."

"Oh my God, you've named them, haven't you?"

"Only the bold ones."

"Jesus. Are you gonna introduce me to your citrus harem or what?"

"I said they had names, I didn't say they were emotionally available."

"Okay, now it's weird."

There was a long, warm pause, like a comfort blanket around me.

"Noah."

"Yeah?"

"I mean it. Thank you."

"I haven't done anything."

"You didn't hang up."

He was quiet for a second, then: "Didn't feel like it."

"Good," I said, sliding down off the counter. "Because I don't want to use up all your goodwill before I get to ask you a favor…"

"I'm not ready for this," I told him.

We were driving towards Dominion of Light, me in my bank-loan outfit with most of the dust beaten back out of it, he with his arm out the window, the wind helping to keep me cool.

"You'll be fine," he said.

"I don't know shit about the Bible."

"Well," he said, deadpan. "It's about this dude called *Jeebus*…"

"I know that much, I just don't know…. Let's just say I'm not chapter and verse."

"Genesis, Exodus… *Leviticus*…?" he guessed.

"I thought a librarian would know things like that."

"I'm not a librarian."

I looked at him.

"You said you were a librarian!"

"I didn't."

"You did!"

"No, you just tracked me down *working* in the library."

Damn. He was right.

"So what is your job, then?"

"I'm an archivist."

"What's the difference?"

"An archivist takes care of the past. A librarian just gives it away to strangers."

I released a slow smile.

"Oooh, that's smart."

"Thanks."

"You had that locked away in that brain of yours, didn'tcha? Waiting for someone to ask."

"I'm an archivist. I have an archive."

We pulled up outside the huge, white building.

The parking lot was bigger than the one at Walmart.

"Do archivists earn more than librarians?"

"Nope."

"A girl's gotta try."

He looked like he was about to kiss me on the cheek. I waited.

"Good luck in there," he said.

I opened the door.

"Okay. Here goes nothing—"

The lobby alone could've housed a Starbucks, a Wendy's, and a modest regional airport. I stood in line for the help desk, staffed by bored teenagers in matching polo shirts—sky blue with that tidy little dove-and-cross logo—until I got sick of it, and decided to look around.

Inside the main auditorium—sorry, the *Worship Dome*—it was like stepping into a Jesus-themed Coachella, except it was too brightly painted and, astonishingly, too big. Springsteen would've struggled to fill the place. Stadium seating, rows and rows. Vast curved video screens flanking the stage. Cameras on robot arms gliding silently overhead, catching every blessed angle of Pastor Joel DuMont as he delivered his holy TED Talk.

"You are *not* the divorce," he said, his voice rich

and buttery, like he gargled caramel sauce. When he put his foot on the edge of the stage, I thought he was about to crowd-surf to the rapture.

"You are *not* the addiction. Not the worst day of your life. Not the guilt you carry in silence. That is not your name. God sees you as healed—even before the healing comes."

The crowd murmured their approval, and up behind him, a twelve-piece band glided into something that sounded like a Coldplay tribute, while the choir sat waiting their turn.

I looked at DuMont's face, looming huge on the screen. He worked hard, I'll give him that. Glistening in sweat.

And then I realized—it was actual glitter.

"Hi there!"

I spun to see a middle-aged woman with a retail smile, dressed in the tour merchandise.

"Need help finding a seat?"

"I'm here for a job interview."

"Oh," she said, laughing brightly, and putting a hand on my arm. "Well… good luck darlin'! This way."

The desk was absurd, a sprawling acre of teak big enough to host a pool tournament. Nothing on the top. No computer, no phone, nothing to interrupt the sense of polished emptiness for all eternity.

But facing outward it was decked out like a carnival float, a festival of ribbons and banners, flags of country and state. The centerpiece was a huge glossy version of the badge they all wore, big as a dinner plate. The dove and the cross.

I'd worn some gaudy shit in my time, but this? This was biblical. I've seen drag queens with more restraint.

I expected DuMont to sweep in with a bottle of tequila, a roadie and a groupie. But when the door opened, it was a small, bald, nondescript object who looked like he advised on pensions.

"Erin Callahan? Good morning, I'm Milton Grieves."

"Oh—hello." I was confused.

He carried a laptop and a slim orange file, which he placed on the desk as he eased himself into the huge leather seat.

"Well," he said, chuckling at the imposition. "We don't often see résumés from—what should we call it—non-members?"

I flashed my best employ-me smile.

"My mom said she'd spoken to the Pastor about it."

"Yes, so he told me. I just want to start by thanking you for coming all the way out here from… where is it you live?"

"East 6th Avenue."

"Oh yes," he said. "My youngest likes the Donut World out there."

My second smile was tighter. Donut World. That's the right place for me. Somewhere you could wipe things down after I left. Not here, where the carpet was deep enough to hide half of my heels.

"Well now. Pastor DuMont is very busy, so he's asked me to speak with you in person about how you could be of service to the Church."

"Okay, but Colleen—that's my mom—she said she'd spoken to the Pastor. In person. That I'd be meeting with the Pastor. In person."

He caught the tone, and gave me a look as if Mom had promised I could watch as DuMont cleaned the toilets.

"The Pastor is preparing to host the Governor and his wife." Like: what the hell did you think? That the guy running the hundred-million-dollar mega-church interviews his own minions? The smug was practically dripping onto his branded, dove-and-cross silk tie.

I slid my tongue into my cheek and tried to count five. But by three I was pissed, and decided to turn on the charm.

"What's the AC bill like in a place like this?"

He blinked. Took a second. Composed himself. When you're doing admin for God, you learn to handle this kind of thing.

"We're a very fortunate ministry," he said with slick assurance. "We have many wonderful donors, from all across Ohio."

"And on TV too?"

"Pastor DuMont likes to reach out to those who cannot reach him in person."

"What, like, lazy people? Or just old?"

He picked up the file and laptop and stood. He had better things to do.

"You might find this amusing Miss Callahan. Many people do, those who had the comfort of being born into faith. But some of us have to fight for faith. We can't do it on the shifting sands of... whatever you people believe in these days. And friendly advice: next time you've got a job interview try not to ask *all* of the questions."

He started to walk away, but I couldn't resist.

"Okay, but just one more question. You're okay with Colleen being Catholic?"

He stopped.

He had to have the last word. Middle management on the up.

Gotcha.

"Strictly, she's a former Catholic. But it doesn't matter. We're proud to be a nondenominational church."

"Is that the kind that welcomes *anybody*?"

"Of course."

"Even, say, Barack Obama."

His smile, when it came, was a feat of engineering.

"All sinners are welcome here."

"Gay sinners too?"

In the last week I'd been stared down by cops, killers, cameras, cheated wives, and the parents of murdered children. This guy? Please.

"Repentance is at the heart of faith."

"Why do they have to repent for being what God

made them?"

"Pastor DuMont is devoted to the scripture."

"And scripture says repent for being gay?"

"It says repent for sins. We are all sinners, aren't we, Erin? This ministry is all about repentance."

He sat again.

"Repentance, revival and restoration."

And he very slowly placed his fingertips on top of the orange file and looked at me, smiling.

I held his gaze.

Held it.

And then I flickered to the file.

What's in there?

"But you're not homosexual, Erin, so the question doesn't arise."

I shifted. "You can't tell by looking, can you? I might be. You never know."

"You'd be amazed what we know. I've been part of this wonderful congregation for four years now, Erin. But the Church of Jesus goes back two *thousand* years. It has a long memory."

He drummed his fingers on the orange file.

"It even has records."

What's in there?

"And your family is part of that history, through your wonderful mother. She's been an important member of this ministry for nearly twenty years. She's given herself to our work here. Tireless. Devoted. So we know a great deal about you and your family."

I could see how these guys could fill a Worship Dome. Even their clerks could leave me pinned to my seat in the house of God. No staring him down now. Now I was just gazing unblinking at the desk, the dove and the cross. When he eventually took his fingers off the file, and I let go of the arms of the chair, he went on like this was a done deal.

"Let's discuss your service to the Church. I understand you'll need a small stipend, and that you have experience with children?"

The pause before experience was needle-fine.

"We have many in our community who need assistance, especially during services. Childcare, help with Bible studies, with guidance. You can help them. And we can continue to help you."

New smile. Same template.

"It's always best," he said softly, "when there's a little give and take."

Baby's Breath

Chapter 15: The Lifeline

"Donut World? You're kidding me."

The car was warm, and the air outside had turned hazy—late-afternoon heat rising off the blacktop in low, visible waves. Noah had the windows cracked, one hand on the wheel, the other draped over the sill, fingers tapping to a song neither of us had bothered to hear.

"Nope," I told him, gazing out the window. "Whole thing was like he was selling me a used car and Jesus combo. Didn't blink once. I think they train for that."

"I guess you weren't buying?"

"I asked if they'd let Obama join the Church."

He looked over and smiled proudly.

But we hadn't spoken since then. I don't think he'd seen me this quiet before. Few had. He kept glancing over uncertainly, like he thought he might've said something wrong and was trying to remember what.

It wasn't him.

I should have told him that, of course. I should have explained the swamp I was wading into before I asked him to drive me straight to the edge. But I didn't have the words, and he didn't have the tools.

So I stayed silent, staring out at the strip malls and storage units and churches sliding by. The signs of America—buy shit you don't need, keep it in a box, and ask forgiveness. Like Grieves demanding mine. Saying *records*, as if my whole life was stored in triplicate and God was reviewing it on a clipboard. The slow, careful way he'd placed his fingertips on that orange file and waited for me to blink.

I didn't want to talk. A stress headache was building up behind my eyes, and I could feel the slow, steady thump of my pulse. I didn't want Noah's good intentions or quiet questions. So I stared out the window, willing the houses to look familiar, the street signs to turn local. Just get me home. Let me be alone.

When we pulled up on Cherry Street, Noah asked, "You sure you're good?" What he meant was, *you're sure I'm not in the shit for something I don't even remember?* It's a woman's superpower, the potency of the silent treatment, but I hadn't intended to blast him with it today. He was just collateral damage. I nodded—*I'm good*—found the flicker of a smile, and went to scale Ray's fence again.

I hadn't even gotten my shoes off before my phone vibrated. Six missed calls, all from Colleen. What difference would one more make? I ignored her.

The levee around me didn't breach. It didn't have to. It just became porous, slowly, sadly leaking in too many places at once to possibly fix. Everything simply drained out. Torrents run downhill. This one was taking me with it.

Whatever was left looked like Erin. Didn't feel like her.

I'd walked into that Church armed to the teeth with sarcasm and walked out with nothing but static in my chest. Maybe I'd been fooling myself. Maybe I never had the strength for this fight. Maybe it was all bravado. In the end, I bent to the will of that bald little asshole—and now I was trapped. My head was thumping.

I wiped my face and looked at my phone. Seven missed calls, and—oh look—two messages too. *Good luck, honey,* and *I can't believe we'll be doing His work together.* No Mom, I can't either. None of us can, least of all Him. This is it now, though. This is my life. Every day I'll head to a job I hate, hoping the presence of innocent kids will fill the guilty space inside me—a begging bowl scooped out the year Dad left, hollowed out by the relentless clawing of Colleen's righteousness. And every evening she'd call to remind me that she and God had conspired to place me in this safe little trap. And she'd scoop the hole out afresh. The thumping behind my eyes wasn't a headache anymore—it was Erin, pounding to get out. To save herself from her mother.

And from her father too. How was I going to track him down if I was on my knees in that goddamn church all day, and on my knees before the altar of Mom every evening? And if I didn't track him down, he'd track me down, and kill me.

The phone rang again. I blew my nose, put my head between my knees, locked on a breezy smile, and answered.

"Hi, Mom!"

"Well?" she said, breathless with expectation. "Tell me everything. Isn't Pastor Joel a wonderful man?"

"No," I told her. "Well, maybe he is, I don't know. It was someone else. An admin guy called Milton something."

"Milton Grieves? Oh, Milton's nice," she said, in the tone of somebody expecting cheesecake and getting a Fig Newton. "So? What did he say? Did you tell him about your teaching certificate?"

"It's not a teaching—" *Oh, what's the point?* "Yeah,

I told him everything."

"And?"

She'd put her chips down for this. Five grand's a lot to gamble on someone like me. I figured I owed her the sales pitch.

"It was good, yeah. It was—he told me all about the cost of the AC, and about the history of the Church. And we kind of agreed that I'd start in two weeks, when—"

I probably didn't need a phone to hear the holler she emitted. It warped sound in my earpiece, and I had to hold it a foot away until she'd died down.

"—when the paperwork is done."

"Oh honey. Oh Erin, I'm so glad you'll be working alongside me! This was meant to be! God has a path for us all, Erin, even when we can't always see it without a little help."

A little help? I get it. This was the moment for me to confirm I would be lost without her, that she had swept to my rescue like some kind of swashbuckling pirate nun, that her sainthood was already in the mail, and that she was the greatest mother since—and potentially including—Mary.

"Yeah, thanks Mom."

There was a beat of silence—then a soft, satisfied sigh.

"This is going to be so good for you," she went on. "It's structure. It's faith. It's healing. You just need to show them who you really are."

"So," I said, showing her who I really was. "Do you want me to come over for the five thousand, or will you write a check, or…?"

"Just give me your Venmo," Colleen said. "I'll transfer it tonight."

"Venmo? I thought we buried that thing back in 2019."

"Oh I don't know about these things. Every five minutes they're inventing something new…"

But I'd stopped listening. Her voice blurred into noise. All I heard was the word: *Venmo*. Something cracked across my mind like glass under pressure—a sudden, blinding flash of possibility.

Venmo.

Garrett.

His Facebook was a dead end. His email was unguessable. No other socials that I could find. But Venmo? People used Venmo all the time before it got a rep for being wildly insecure, and having more bugs than a hobo's vest. In the old days, you had to choose—actively *choose*—whether your transactions were private, or whether you preferred to let every law enforcement agency on the planet see all the illegal shit you were doing. Plenty of people forgot to tick the *Keep This Private* box, and eventually Venmo changed how it worked. But if Garrett had used it way back, maybe his transactions were still public...

"Mom," I said, holding my phone in front of my mouth so I could see the screen, "I need to reinstall Venmo, let me call you back, or just send the cash later. Gotta go. Thanks for the job and all that shit—"

I hung up, already opening the store. The download was fast. Erin never used Venmo, but Helen did all the time, back in the day. Tasha took payments that way, so did Darnell. I logged in with my hcalley236@gmail.com account, reset the password, and ignored the welcome screen.

I went straight to the search bar.

Name, @username, phone, or email.

Into my contacts. Search *Dad*. There it is, the number he'd called from three Christmases ago, the one I'd only kept so I could taunt Colleen. I pasted it in, stared at it—thumb hovering, heart ticking.

A profile popped up.

Garrett Callahan
@GarrettRidesAgain

God, what a stupid username. But that photo—it was cut out from the only one I had of him, sat on my yellow dresser. An old blurry lake photo from the waist of some boat, water, sky, and a flannel shirt.

I tapped his name.

Public transactions. I almost laughed. It was like he *wanted* to be found.

There were five entries. The first one looked promising—a small transaction from four months ago:

Battery $139.

I clicked through, heart rising, but the sender's name was locked down—*Private*. No location, no notes, nothing beyond that single word.

Okay, nothing to worry about, four more to go.

The second transaction was for "Beer run 🍺". I didn't know what I expected to discover from a beer run, but it turned out to be nothing at all—the same story. A secretive seller and a dead end.

The third read:

> ### $185 to Luanne H.
> ### Memo: Propane delivery.

It was dated eight months ago. A lot can happen in eight months, but it was worth a try. I clicked the seller's name—this time it wasn't hidden, which was progress of sorts. She went by @TugForkQueen. A round-faced woman in a grainy photo, who seemed to survive by selling groceries, gas, and splitting utility bills. One entry said *"re: cleanup and garage"*, which told me nothing. My third dead end.

My pulse hadn't changed speed, but now it had shifted from excited to anxious.

C'mon, c'mon.

On to the next one, which showed somebody had sold my dad *12 x timber*, but had kept all other details private. This was telling me nothing, and West Virginia is a hell of a large area to search one person at a time.

I clicked the last entry and then stopped.

Wait.

West Virginia?

Something in the back of my mind…

Demko said my dad was in West Virginia…

Wasn't there a Tug Fork in West Virginia?

I'd seen it on a map in my classroom. It's a river, down in the south somewhere. They have one called Dismal right next to it, and Fran and I always laughed.

I clicked back to transaction number three.

@TugForkQueen.

Luanne's emojis—a gun, a flag and a heart.

That's like the unofficial logo of West Virginia.

And who buys propane? People in trailer parks. That's not selling beer and wood to a passer-by, that's selling vital supplies to a resident.

And all of it public.

Thank fuck for old folks. Scammers would be lost without them.

I switched to Google.

Tug Fork propane delivery Luanne.

First hit:

Tug Fork River Trailer Park
Williamson, West Virginia.

I locked my phone and stared at the black screen. My hands were shaking. I unlocked it again and took a screenshot, my heart pounding. That was him. That's where he lived, or at least, that's where he was eight months ago. And he'd planned to stick around long enough to order propane. I had no idea how long a propane tank lasted—weeks? Months? Whatever it was, he'd meant to stay.

I called Colleen back.

"Okay," I said, my voice as clean as a newly sharpened knife. "I've got it. You can send the cash over now."

She asked for my username. I gave it. And my heart stepped forward.

I had money, motivation, and the start of a map. I was back on the trail.

Baby's Breath

Chapter 16: The Loaner

Tug Fork River Trailer Park. It sounded like a slur and a punchline, but it was both: a promise and a threat. It sounded made-up, like a setting from a bootleg horror movie. A red flag on a map. Where ghosts live.

But it was real. I Googled the place—it even had its own website, a single page that boasted of convenient access to shopping and dining. It was last updated in 2022. It must have been a year of ups and downs, because there were little banners advertising a "Community Yard Sale and Father's Day Giveaway", followed by a "Spring Cleanup Event".

I checked photos, in case he was there, sitting on a lawn chair, selling off his old crap in front of one of the slatted trailers, or maybe making use of the brown voids where somebody's prefab dream had finally fallen apart and been hauled off on a flatbed.

Hey, at least when they repossessed my home, it would stay where it always was.

I could now ward off that prospect for a little

longer, but five thousand dollars isn't what it used to be. It's not a life-changing sum; it's a life-saving one. Wolves had been at my door long before the media jackals got here.

So before I could even think about finding my father, I had to deal with adult shit.

I sat at my kitchen counter, hunched over the small, bright screen of my new phone, and faced the music. My laptop, my only real tool for managing a life, was still in my classroom—locked behind a police cordon, practically on the moon. So I tapped and swiped my way through a digital minefield.

My gas bill, flagged with a belligerent, all-caps PAST DUE, was first. I navigated the clunky interface of the utility company's mobile site, thumb fumbling at the tiny keyboard, and paid it in full. I watched the number in my banking app shrink with a wince. Next, the minimum payment on my credit card, a grudging tribute to a debt that felt like a life sentence. Water. Student loans, the ghost that never stops haunting. Click, swipe, confirm. With every transaction, a little bit of the pressure eased, and a little bit of my freedom disappeared.

I contemplated paying the cable and internet, a bundle that had once felt impossible to live without. But I wasn't planning on being here for—who knows? It might only be a couple of days, but it could take weeks to find him. Tug Fork might be the end of a path, or the start of one.

Or he might find me first, and I'd never come home.

I decided not to pay my cable bill. Let them chase me for the cash in my grave.

Even so, by the time I was done, the five grand was closer to two. It had never been enough to buy a reliable car, and now it wasn't enough to buy an unreliable one. Renting was an option, but a costly one, a slow bleed that would drain me dry. And it left a paper trail a mile wide, a set of receipts Demko could trace from Lancaster to wherever I ended up. No: renting was the last resort. I needed a loaner.

Noah's car was out of the question. It was a piece of junk, for one thing, and for another, he needed it. He had a job, a life that wasn't currently imploding. Dragging him further into my mess felt wrong, even if he'd offered.

No way I could tell Colleen I needed a car so I could leave town—not right after I'd fleeced her for five grand.

Maybe there was some way to get hold of the keys to Eddie's car, but I didn't know how. Break in? I didn't have any idea how to do that. And I didn't have time to watch some cat burglar movie for ideas.

That left one person. One terrible, reckless, last-ditch idea.

Ty Holcomb.

He had access to cars. Dozens of them. And I had leverage. Or at least, Helen had leverage, before someone tried to put a bullet through his skull. Lomax said he was at home, sedated. That complicated things. But it didn't make them impossible.

It just meant I'd have to get creative.

The Uber dropped me at the end of Ty's street, and I tried to get my bearings. I'd only been here once—we usually did it at my place—and although it looked familiar, I wasn't totally sure which door I was about to knock on.

His neighborhood was all neat hedges and cracked driveways, the kind of place where every house had two cars and a fridge held shut with duct tape. Anxiety and gentrification, locked in a slow, silent war. Every lawn was mowed, but every other roof needed patching. It was a neighborhood holding its breath, praying the property values would go up before the foundations gave out.

Chapter 23: The Homecoming

It could get away with that in darkness, which was the only time I'd seen it. Now, in the bright, unforgiving light of day, all the houses looked the same. I walked the length of the street, then turned and walked back, trying to place the driveway. I was so focused on the houses that I didn't notice the curtain twitch in one of them.

I'd just settled on a two-story colonial with a peeling porch when the door cracked open in the next one along. Ty's face appeared in the gap, pale and drawn. He looked like he hadn't slept in a week.

"What the fuck, Helen?" he hissed, his voice a panicked whisper. "My *fucking wife* is here!"

Okay, so that's the house. I squared my shoulders, put on my game face, and gave him a full set of teeth, clean as a flight attendant. He'd only met Helen in the past, so even on the best of days the appearance of the real me—Erin—would have confused the poor sap. But now? Not even I knew who this new version was. I pitched my voice to theater levels, letting it carry just enough to be overheard by someone inside.

"Good afternoon. I'm here on behalf of Cedar Ridge Elementary. My name is Erin Callahan."

He blinked like a dog being shown a card trick. I stepped up the path, fixing him with a meaningful stare.

"You will be aware we had a terrible incident earlier this month," I continued, channeling the weaponized empathy I'd heard from Greevy. "And I've been told that in the past, you've been a very generous supporter of the school community."

"I—*what?*"

Meaningful stares are lost on Tyler Holcomb.

"I realize this is an imposition, especially at such a difficult time for you and your family," I said, tilting my head with faux deference and slightly widening my eyes. *Understand me, you dumbass.* "But we were hoping you might be willing to help us again. We need to borrow a vehicle. Just for a few days. To better support those affected."

The door swung open wider, and there she was—slim, polished, radiating suspicion like it was a skincare product. She had a dish towel in one hand and a look of weary disdain etched permanently into the set of her mouth. So this was Paige. She looked from Ty's scrambled face to mine—calm, professional, scrubbed clean of everything but fundraising charm.

"Ty," she said, in a voice trained in justifiable suspicion. "Who's this?"

I stepped forward, extending a hand, watching

him try to dissolve into the drywall as the fuse hissed down to his own detonation.

"Paige Holcomb? I'm so sorry to intrude. My name is Erin Callahan—I work at Cedar Ridge. I was just explaining to your husband, we're in a very difficult position right now."

Paige ignored my hand. She crossed her arms, her gaze sweeping over me, taking me in. I'd prepped for this. The bland, competent, lend-me-money suit, the one that screamed: "I have a 401k and I'm not afraid to use it." Shoes that could stand a day in a classroom. Not a seducer, not a rival, not a threat, not a suspect. I was a representative. I was an institution.

And sure, I was a bit of a blackmailer too.

Ty looked like his eyeballs were trying to escape.

"Oh, right, difficult position," she repeated, looking entirely at him, her voice laced with ice. "Another, Ty? While the kids are home?"

But—*oh, I was good*—I was already in motion, my unwavering professional smile cracking just a touch. If I'd owned pearls, I'd have clutched them.

"I don't know what you're suggesting, but I'm here on behalf of the school—a school that's suffered a terrible tragedy, and which is asking previous benefactors if they'd be kind enough to—"

"Don't give me that shit, bitch."

Okay, I was good, but I might not be *that* good.

Ty, from his position being eaten by shadows, said, "It's true, Paige. Me and Arnie loan the school cars for…"

He was already out of ideas, so I stepped in.

"Arnie and your husband have been wonderful."

A silence.

"Ask Arnie, if you're not sure. Ask Principal Greevy at the school. I have her number." I started reaching into my *fundraising-gala* handbag, but she stopped me with a raised palm.

"Last time it was a yoga professional. Downward dog my ass."

"Mrs. Holcomb," I said, reason itself. "If I were that kind of woman, do you honestly believe I'd be standing on your doorstep, in broad daylight, asking to speak to your *husband's wife*?"

I let the question hang in the air. Paige's expression didn't change, but I saw a flicker of something else. Doubt?

"Your husband—Mr. Holcomb," I corrected myself, turning my performance to her, "He and his employers have been very kind to the school in the past. He's loaned us vehicles for field trips, for fundraising drives, even to help transport equipment for accessibility programs. He has been a real pillar of support. And now, with so many families struggling, with staff displaced and unable to get around, we're reaching out to the most trusted people in our community. His name—and yours—were at the top of our list."

I'd like to thank The Academy. I had the conviction of a true believer. I was no longer a homewrecker; I was a public servant, a woman on a mission of mercy. Even Ty looked like he believed me.

"I'm telling you Paige," he said, "we even put your name on it, and Arnie put Betty and the kids on it."

Nice touch.

Paige was silent for a long moment, studying my face. I was granite.

"There are tax benefits too. I can arrange for the school to send you a brochure on it."

She looked me up and down one last time, a long, appraising stare. I couldn't tell if she believed my story, or if she'd just decided she didn't care.

"You need a car?" she said, her voice suddenly all business.

I nodded. "Just for a few days. To help with the

families. We'd be so grateful. Any car from the lot would be—"

"No, take mine."

What the fuck? I thought. *What is this? Just twisting the knife in Ty?*

"Ty, get my keys."

He blinked. "What the fuck?"

Yep, there goes the knife.

She turned on him with a look that could melt paint. He vanished into the house, and she turned back to me, continuing in the same voice, cold and sour like unsweetened tea. By the time Ty ran back, clutching the keys and his sanity, I had no idea how to cope with any of this anymore.

"It's only a compact," she said, "The blue Corolla. It'll need gas. Don't smoke in it. And bring it back when you're done with your… community outreach."

And she dropped the keys onto the path in front of me like a used tissue, turned on her heel, and shut the door with a studied, controlled click.

"Thank you," I said, my voice barely a whisper, but trying to maintain. Sweat trickled between my shoulder blades as I bent to pick up the fob.

As I unlocked the car I heard her voice, as brass

as a bell: "Tyler Holcomb, you get in here. We're not finished."

Baby's Breath

Chapter 17: The Goat

US-33 took me south out of Lancaster, past the strip malls and gas stations, into the straightforward geometry of Ohio farmland. Green squares of corn and soy, neat white houses, the world laid out in a sensible grid.

Everything here knew its purpose. The highway barely took a curve, and I barely had to think. My mind wandered to the black box of the interrogation. The road here, in the neat structure of Ohio, felt as logical and direct as the case Demko had laid against my father. But the accusations didn't fit. That wasn't the Dad I remembered: the boogeyman they'd built in Interview Room Four. Down that twisting, broken road in the mountains ahead, I hoped I'd find the truth.

Somewhere after Athens and the Hocking River, the landscape began to buckle. The neat grid fractured. The road narrowed, twisting to meet the foothills of Appalachia. Hills rose up, dense with oak and hickory, their summer leaves so thick they seemed to suck the light out of the air. The road became a tight, winding, writhing thing. The world was no longer a map; it was a maze, a place of blind corners and sudden, plunging valleys where the sun couldn't reach.

By the time I crossed the Ohio River into West Virginia, the wilting heat was heavy with the sweet, rotten smell of damp earth and fallen apples left too long in the sun. Signs for towns became fewer, replaced by hand-painted boards advertising Pentecostal revivals and pick-your-own farms. The houses seemed to shrink, cowering closer to the road, with porches haunted by the ghosts of broken machinery. This wasn't a place where things got fixed; it was a place where things were left to decay, swallowed by the kudzu and the dank, ancient decrepitude of the mountains.

Twenty miles to Tug Fork, and the land felt like it was closing in on me. The trees leaned over the road, ducking away from the danger of the lower slopes, their canopy throwing a perpetual twilight. This felt like the damp cellar of the country, where the sun didn't shine and the rules didn't apply and only the lucky got out.

I was heading towards a confrontation with something more memory than reality, and every curve in the road felt like it was pulling me deeper into a place where anything could happen.

I was halfway through Prospect Creek before I

even realized it was a town—struggling to read my phone while keeping one eye on the snaking road. Somewhere around here was the turn-off for Tug Fork Trailer Park, but where?

I pulled over between a low, dusty building and a sagging animal enclosure topped with barbed wire. Maybe they'd know at the house?

Stepping out of the air-conditioned car was like being slapped with a hot, wet towel. The heat mauled you. Even the insects had checked out for the afternoon: the cicadas mute, the usual buzz of crickets silenced. You could almost hear them gasping in the brittle grasses, clinging to stalks that crackled like dry paper.

I knocked and called out, but there was no answer at the door, and I was just about to head back in gratitude to the cool interior of Paige's car when I heard an unearthly shriek.

"*Naaah!*"

Took me a moment to locate the source: a small, fat, coarse-coated goat baking in the sun. He'd managed to shove his head through one of the six-inch squares in the fence, and then his backward-curving horns had become trapped in the wire. Next to his head, a hand-painted sign on the fence simply read: STANLEY. I assumed the goat, not the owner.

"It's okay, Stanley, I gotcha," I said in the sooth-
ing voice I'd perfected for crying children, and
braced myself for the simple task of grabbing his
horns, twisting and pushing him back to freedom.

"*Naaah!*" screamed Stanley, and locked his foothold in absolute defiance.

I pulled him forwards to free the horns. He
rammed me hard, then slumped right back where he
started.

"Work with me here, buddy."

"*Naaah!*" he screamed again, and gazed venom-
ously up at me with a single eye, like a letterbox into
pure idiocy.

I bent my knees for another attempt, discover-
ing in real-time that goats are surprisingly strong
and unsurprisingly stubborn. I tried to reverse him
toward freedom, he insisted on headbutting himself
back into captivity. We did two laborious minutes of
this before, by mutual consent, we decided to take a
break.

"Jesus, Stanley," I gasped, doubled over. "How
are you not extinct?"

I wiped sweat from my brow, neck and chest,
and gripped his horns tight again, readying myself
to hold and maneuver. This time he waited patiently
until he was almost entirely free—and only then

headbutted his rescuer, planting himself right back in the trap.

"Is he stuck again?" called a voice from behind me, raspy and amused. A thick, squat woman in her seventies, as truculent as the goat, was marching from around the back of the house with bare legs erupting from a smock, shoving her knitting into her pocket.

"I'm not used to this kind of thing," I panted.

"Nobody gets used to Stanley."

"Yeah, I'm starting to see that."

She gripped him with a roughness I wouldn't have thought legal—wrestling him, twisting him, and finally hurling him two feet backwards. He turned side-on, rotated his mouthful of grim teeth, and went back to chewing the few spindly twigs that survived the rocks.

She turned to me. "Thanks for tryin'."

"No problem."

"Need some Oxy?"

I held my gaze and my expression.

"*Naaah!*" said Stanley.

"I'm sellin'," she said.

"I'm good for now, thanks. I'm a bit too...

busy… I'm trying to find my dad. He lives around here, I think."

"Whereabouts?" like we were picking up where we left off with the goat, and I'd just hallucinated the low-grade opiate dealing.

"Tug Fork Trailer Park."

She was nodding before I'd finished. "Half a mile back, on your right. I'd say you can't miss it, but you can. Sign blew down back in the '22 storm."

I walked back to my car.

I'd come here to face off against a monster. Ended up wrangling livestock with a geriatric Tony Montana.

Chapter 18: The Park

The sign had rotted to a joke—two rusted poles, brutally severed, and a moss-ridden wooden sign, being slowly strangled by kudzu vine. Of the site's name, only the letters TUG were still visible, once proudly red, now weathered to the tone of a rotting peach. Some wit had vandalized it with a drawing of a hand pulling on a cock and balls. It was less a welcome and more an epitaph.

I turned off the main road and onto a track of spitting gravel that snaked between a rats-nest of trees and vines, until it opened on a clearing full of trailers perched on cinder blocks, their metal skins weeping rust beneath the relentless West Virginia sun.

I'd seen a couple of pictures online—too grainy to trust, too hopeful to believe—but this? This was a masterclass in decay. It was a museum of forgotten things: pickup trucks returning to the earth, the skeletal remains of swing sets, the echoes of barbecues long gone cold.

Half the lots were empty, just brown, rectangular scars in the dirt, like shallow graves over the corpses of dreams. Of those remaining, most had windows caked opaque in dust outside, and grease inside. Several had shattered glass or doors hanging off hinges. Only a handful looked lived in. At least, I hoped nobody lived in the rest.

I killed the engine and the silence that rushed in was absolute. Even the birds seemed to have checked out. This wasn't just a place of poverty; it was a place of profound, soul-deep exhaustion. The air smelled of damp particleboard and resignation, like somebody's unfinished cry. I had hoped, in some stupid, secret corner of my heart, that I would get here and find it was all a mistake. That the Venmo trail belonged to a different Garrett Callahan. That somehow the father I remembered—the one from before all the killings—wasn't this man. That what I remembered as a patient, reliable, borderline-respectable man had found somewhere better than this to live.

I started with the trailer closest to the entrance, a single-wide with foil taped over the windows. No answer. The next had a dog that threw itself against the door with such fury I thought the flimsy aluminum might buckle. I backed away slowly.

At the third trailer, an ancient woman opened the door, her face as pinched and brown as a dried apple. I told her who I was, and who I was looking for. She smiled, helpful, hopeful and, it was immediately clear, demented. She told me her name—Margaret—and said her father would know when he came home. I thanked her, and moved on.

I crossed four consecutive empty lots—the dried, dead grass crackling sharply under my feet, and then to the next trailer. At least this looked like it was cared for, a little. It was bigger than the others, a double-wide that might have been nice twenty years ago. The owner, or tenant, or prisoner, had done his best to keep it together until his lottery numbers came up and he had a chance in life. Taped to the inside of the window was a red, white, and blue poster.

MAKE AMERICA GREAT AGAIN.

Looking around at the skeletal remains of the American dream, I didn't envy whoever got stuck with that task.

I knocked, a curtain moved, and after a long moment, the door creaked open. The man inside seemed like an undertaker from a silent movie. Long, bent and mournful—pitying the dead and judging the living, entirely the wrong way around. His small, suspicious eyes took me in.

"Whatever it is, I'm not in the market."

"No, I'm not selling anything, I'm just looking for somebody."

He took a step forward and looked where I'd parked, ten lots away. "Can't park there, honey, that's the Cready spot."

"Sorry, I'll move it in a moment. Listen, I'm sorry to bother you, but I'm looking for Garrett Callahan? I was told he lived around here."

"Sure, right there. Number fourteen."

He pointed. It was the next trailer along, diagonally on the other side of the grassy path. My mouth went dry, and I stared.

"He's not home though."

"Sorry?" I said, and looked back at him.

"He's not home."

"I'm his daughter," I told him. "Erin. I'm—we lost touch, I haven't seen him in years. But I'm trying to get hold of him. Any idea when he'll be back?"

If I was quick, maybe I could call the police. But what would I even tell them?

"He ain't here," he said. "Moved on."

"Oh." The word came out as a puff of air. The disappointment was a physical thing, a confirmation of a truth I didn't want. My shoulders slumped. "Do you know where he went? It's important."

"Owe you money, does he?"

"No, it's not that—"

"Owes me money. Seventy dollars. And a drill bit."

"I'm… listen, I'll try to talk to him about that if I can find him. Did he say where he'd gone?"

He chewed on that for a moment, his gaze drifting to the empty lot across from his trailer. "He was a good neighbor. Fixed my step after the storm a while back, but otherwise kept to himself." He looked back at me, his expression hardening. "Couldn't find no work, though. Not around here."

He stepped off the trailer and leaned closer. "He was in trouble, you know. Up north. I heard he had a police record."

He said it as a statement, but it was a question. He was testing me. I widened my eyes just enough—practiced innocence. "A record? What for?"

He shrugged, a gesture that said *not my business, but I'm making it my business.* "Heard it was something with his wife, some kind of scandal. I heard rumors, but I never listen to rumors. Hate people who spread 'em. But folks find out. Makes it hard to get on."

"Right," I said, my voice hollow. "So, you don't

Baby's Breath

know anything about where he is?"

"Don't think so."

"Okay. Well… thanks anyway."

I turned away, the gravel crunching under my sensible shoes, my last hope draining into the dirt. There was no relief here, no exoneration. Just the quiet, damning confirmation of a broken life. Perhaps I could come back later, break in to number 14, look for clues—I was wondering how to do that when…

"He went back, I heard," said a new voice. I turned. It was the man's wife, standing in the doorway to the trailer.

I walked closer, but before I heard the answer— before I even asked the question—resignation settled on me like a layer of silt.

"Back where?"

"Ohio," she said. "Where he came from. Lancaster way. He told me he had some business up there."

"What kind of business?"

"Couldn't tell you. People have unfinished business, I guess. Hope that helps you."

The words didn't land with a shock. There was no fresh wave of emotion. Just a deep, weary acceptance. *Unfinished business.* Of course. This was the man who had shot up my classroom, who had left flowers on my doorstep, a note that damned us both. This was the path he set me on. The hope I'd secretly harbored—the one where this was all a terrible mistake—died right there on that gravel track. What replaced it wasn't fear. It was cold, and hard, and final.

I had to find him. For Della. For all of them.

And for myself.

I looked at my father's trailer. Its windows were coated in decay. A propane can, maybe Luanne's propane can, was on its side at the end of the lot.

I turned back to the couple, my posture straighter now.

"Did he say anything else? Where he might be working? A friend's name?"

The undertaker had had enough, and stalked back indoors. His wife stayed. "He didn't say anything to me, sweetheart. I'm sorry. Maybe to someone else. Just packed his truck one morning, and was gone. Good luck to him, I say. Place like this…"

I nodded, a single, sharp gesture of understanding. "Thanks for your time."

I walked back to the car, my steps measured and

deliberate now. I glanced back at his trailer one last time. There'd be no clues in there, even if I could somehow break in without the neighbors hearing. That dusty box was a skeleton of a life, picked clean. It held no answers. No justice. Just rust and grime and a sun-bleached door.

The mission hadn't changed, but I had. The hope was gone. In its place, a grim determination had taken root.

Chapter 19: The Queen

I'd pulled over to think in the stifling heat of Paige Holcomb's Corolla, the engine and AC off—idling felt like a luxury I couldn't afford.

I regretted it immediately. With the windows closed, the air inside already felt thick, stale and second-hand. Cracking the window only invited the heat in—angry, wet, and immediate. It shoved me down in my seat and wrung me out in seconds.

I'd driven out of the trailer park and pulled over at the end of the turn-out, by the busted sign, silently jacking off at me from the weeds. The road ahead was as mute and drained as the park behind me. An occasional car or truck drawing deep breaths as it swept past me, and then stillness and heat.

My father had been here. I was sure of that much. He had smelled this same defeated air, and now he was gone—back to Ohio, on *unfinished business.*

That phrase came laden with too many trashy novels and bad mafia movies. Maybe it just meant a carpenter going back to tie off an old construction contract. A job he hadn't finished.

Or it could mean a grudge left to rot in this heat. A man who'd had eighteen years in the wilderness to let his frustrations and betrayals ferment into something diabolical and grotesque. Demko's flat, certain stare was hard to argue with. The DNA on my phone, harder still. It was an anchor, dragging the whole rotting story to the bottom.

And yet... it didn't fit. I felt like I was trying to solve a puzzle with pieces from the wrong box. That man—the one the cops built for me in Interview Room Four—cold, calculating, maniacal— that wasn't my father. That was a stranger. The man I'd known smelled of sawdust, and his rough hands were gentle when he lifted me. He drank Folgers in the morning and Bud after dark. Sat in tired work clothes at six p.m., reading the paper while Mom made dinner. His shoes were as worn and soft as he was. He built things. Mended things. Smoothed wood, shaved off splinters. That's not a man who unleashes hell in a classroom one afternoon, and then takes photos of his daughter's breakdown to entertain Twitter.

But that good, sane man lived eighteen years ago. Think how much a child changes in that time. How much could an adult? That's a whole lifetime. Was I still that same girl—the one who bent to Colleen's will, while her father was taken away in cuffs?

It nearly broke me.

Maybe it broke him too.

What if the Garrett Callahan I remembered was just another ghost, a fond, faded memory of someone who didn't exist anymore? I was chasing a man I hadn't even known for half my life. And I was doing it in a place outside of time—a forgotten fold in the map where things came to die.

I had to find someone who knew him *now*. Not *then*. *Then* told me nothing. The residents here were blanks. Margaret, sweet and lost in the fog of her own mind. The mournful undertaker, staring at the seventy bucks and the drill bit Dad owed him, like that was the sum total of a man's life. They measured him in debts and vague scandals. No memory. No warmth. Just wreckage.

One name left. A flimsy digital thread from a world away: Luanne, @TugForkQueen. The propane drop.

It was probably nothing. One transaction. Maybe she'd squinted at him in the sun, taken his cash, and forgotten him before he even drove away. But maybe he was a regular. Someone she passed a few minutes with while the tanks switched out. Maybe he'd said something. Maybe she had a clue.

Or maybe she just knew to steer clear of the crazy guy in trailer fourteen.

Even as I talked myself into it, I knew it felt thin. What did I know about the girl who rang me up at Kroger? Or the guy who bagged the onions? Nothing. I only knew their names because they were written on a badge.

But Luanne—whoever she was—was all I had. And chasing her felt like defiance. Like standing up to the gravity of this place. It gave me purpose.

My fingers felt clumsy and slick with sweat as I opened the Venmo app again. I navigated to her profile: the gun, the flag, the heart. The Holy Trinity of these mountains.

I hit *Request Payment*, typed in a dollar, and added a note.

Need propane. Can you help?

The request posted with a green check, the note sitting awkwardly beside a payment I didn't expect her to fulfill. I dropped the phone on the passenger seat, the screen still glowing.

Now, there was nothing to do but wait. I leaned my head back against the seat, the cheap fabric already damp. Through the dusty windshield, the main road shimmered in the heat. A logging truck rumbled past, shaking the ground. An old Ford, loose-jointed and jangling as it passed. And then the marker of gym bro affluence around here—a big Ram 1500 Warlock, vivid blue, with an aftermarket exhaust that let out a low, rattling growl, bruising the air it passed through. It swept by the turn-off for the trailer park, heading west.

Every town had one. Big truck, big mouth, small... self-worth.

A minute later, it passed again, going the other way, back east. It was slower this time. I felt, more than saw, the driver's head turn, a glance towards the dilapidated TUG sign and my little blue car tucked just behind it.

Well, at least it's not just me who gets lost on these signless, aimless roads.

Then it came back, third pass, this time going west again. Moving at a crawl now, the growl of its engine a low thrum that vibrated through the floor of my car. I instinctively slouched down in my seat, my heart giving a hard, single thump against my ribs. The windows were tinted, a dark, impenetrable sheen. I couldn't see the driver. It passed my turn-off and continued down the road for about half a mile, then I saw its brake lights flash red against the asphalt.

It began a laborious turn—either the driver couldn't handle the beast, or the road down there was too narrow. His three-point turn became a five-point, and then a seven, him battling to spin it around, creeping in and out of the dried grasses on the verge. The slowness was deliberate, a mechanical maneuver that felt less like a correction and more like a declaration. He was coming back.

The cheap excuses evaporated, leaving a cold, hard knot of fear in my stomach. This wasn't a coincidence.

My pulse was up, my last nerve twitching when the phone buzzed on the seat beside me, making me leap, the sound a shocking violation of the tense silence.

Luanne.

Where and when?

Relief, vivid and blinding, washed over me. An escape. And a lead. I didn't have time to process the truck; I had to move. I sent her another dollar, with the note:

I'll come to you. Can you send an address?

As I waited, I stared down the road. Seven-point turn had done it. The blue Ram was heading back in my direction, slowly. A predator on a casual patrol. I looked at the phone.

C'mon, c'mon, c'mon, c'mon...

The reply came, a pin dropped on a map, a life raft.

98 Coal Run Spur
Matewan, WV 25678

I didn't hesitate. I jammed the key in the ignition, and Paige's Corolla coughed to life, its tinny engine sounding pathetic and frail. I pulled out, headed straight for the truck. As we passed, fear surged— then broke into something hot and sharp: exhilaration.

A mile on, I pulled over, got my phone out and checked the directions to Coal Run Spur. I'd been so busy getting away from that Ram that I'd set off the wrong way—didn't matter. Might have been nothing anyway, just some guy looking for a dead-end trailer park. Just some guy. In a fifty-thousand-dollar pickup with custom exhausts.

Sure.

Still, in my compact I could maneuver more easily, and I swung around and headed back along the same road, heading for Matewan.

As I rounded the next bend, he was coming right for me again. No doubt now. I put my foot down. We sped past one another once more, and I saw his taillights come on before the landscape warped the road again, and I lost him.

Coal Run Spur was a desolate tunnel carved through a dense, suffocating canopy of trees that pressed down like breathless thoughts. My hands slithered on the steering wheel, and I tried to calm myself.

No way the Ram saw me take this turnoff. No way he could guess where I was going. In these trees, I was invisible. I could sit here till sundown if I had to. I stopped, out of sight of the main road, and took long breaths in the luxury of the air conditioning, lifting my hair from my damp neck.

When I was sure I was alone, I pressed my foot down, the small car whining in protest as it climbed a steep, washboard grade.

I'd told myself I was safe here, but I still almost sobbed with relief when I reached the rusted mailbox, hanging sideways off its post. I swung into a dirt driveway, the car bottoming out with a sickening scrape. Luanne's place was a monument to surrender. A lopsided house with paint peeling off in leprous sheets, and a yard choked with appliances. Some were rusted beyond repair. Some half-fixed. Others bore handwritten prices on curled tape, black marker scrawled across them. A heavy, chain-link cage sagged under a tree, where dozens of propane tanks were stacked like dormant, metallic bombs.

As I killed the engine, a woman emerged from the house. Luanne was unmistakable from her grainy Venmo picture, but the reality was harsher. Her hair hung in limp, oily strands, thinning at the roots. Her skin had the waxy pallor of someone who lived indoors with the curtains drawn, and the area around her mouth was a mess of chapped sores. Whatever she'd succumbed to, alone in these hills, it had decided to take her face before it took her life.

I climbed out of the car slowly, expecting her to move the same way in this liquid heat. But she closed the space between us fast, twitchy and wired. Before I could react, her hand, cold and clammy, landed on my arm.

"You the propane girl?"

"Yeah, that's me," I said, and she took her hand off me and listened to sounds in the distance. I turned too.

The Ram growled somewhere down the hill—a threat with no shape.

Her milk-glass stare snapped into focus, eyes darting toward the noise. I knew how she felt—my own heart seized in my chest. We stood, the two of us, like statues as the rumbling exhaust sounds grew, grew... and then faded.

Then we slid back into the present. Her anxiety—formless, senseless—eased back into that glass stare. Mine—certain, rational—burrowed deeper, curling in my gut, anticipating my return to the road.

"So then..." said Luanne, rubbing her nose with the back of her hand.

I knew I might have to buy the useless fuel if I wanted to get anything out of her, but I was watching every dime. Maybe I'd just try asking first...

"Listen," I said, whispering as if I was afraid the Ram might still hear me. She leaned in, used to shady deals. "Buddy of mine said you had the best deals on propane."

"That's right," she said, and set off in a hurry to

the tanks in their locked cage.

"Thing is," I said, catching up, "I've lost touch with this guy, and I wondered if you know him. He's a family friend. This isn't bad news for him, I just need to find him. Garrett Callahan."

Her face lit up. "Oh sure—I know Garrett! We used to hang out sometimes. Not like that. Well," she chuckled, "sometimes like that. Good man. You seen him?"

"No," I said, "I was hoping you had. He's my dad."

The change was immediate and overwhelming. She lunged forward, wrapping me in a hug that smelled of stale menthols and something vaguely sour, like spoiled milk. "Oh, honey," she whispered, her voice thick with emotion. "I feel like we just understand each other, you and me. Like we're kindred spirits."

I awkwardly patted her back, feeling the sharp, bird-like knobs of her spine through her thin t-shirt. Her performance was exhausting, but I was too close to stop.

She pulled back and started tapping her pockets, looking around. I recognized the signs and pulled out my cigarettes. I lit hers and then mine, and let the camaraderie grow, hoping it would blossom into a fresh lead.

"Luanne," I said, gently easing back into the conversation. "I met with some folks at the trailer park, and they told me he left for Ohio."

"Uh-huh," she nodded.

"On 'unfinished business', they said."

Her eyes narrowed. "Yeah, I bet I know who told you that. Fuckin' Cready. Man don't know shit."

"I didn't buy it either." I hoped I'd found an opening, but she just stood and smoked in silence for ten long seconds.

"'Bout that propane," she said.

Shit. Fine. Okay, let's do this.

The transaction was a clumsy, pathetic dance. It cost me forty dollars of money I couldn't spare. She insisted I stand aside while she loaded the heavy, rusted cylinder into the back of Paige's clean Corolla, where it landed with a loud thud, sitting there, as dense and welcome as a tumor. The whole time, she chattered, her thoughts darting like panicked birds. With the money in her hand, she was suddenly my best friend.

"So," I said, leaning against the car door, trying to seem casual while I made one more attempt. "You knew my dad well?"

"No secrets between us," she said, her voice turned sly, secretive and proud. "Told me the whole thing. Unfinished business my ass. He told me plain as day—had to go back up north to take care of his girl." Her eyes lit up and focused on me. "That's you!" she said, and then slid back to the angry, prideful mumble. "He said his ex-wife was nothing but trouble, always makin' shit up. Wanted to go back to Ohio and look after his blood."

I stared at her. How much of this was real? Her chapped lips sucked on the last of the cigarette and she hurled the butt into the woods, well away from the propane tanks. That much, at least, was sane. Everything else…?

Now I had two stories, two Garretts, at war in my mind. One was a monster, a threat, maybe waiting for me on the road through the woods. He was made of hard evidence, a huge blue truck, a gun, and DNA on a phone. He'd stood in front of me and Della Morrison, with his sleeves rolled up, and got down to business. Unfinished business.

The other Garrett was Luanne's version, delivered through a fog of chemicals and loneliness. This man was protecting his daughter and sleeping with addicts, building McMansions in prestige Lancaster, and haggling for gas on dirt roads. It made no sense at all, but it was a life raft. A life raft made of splinters. An addict's ramblings, or an old man's desperate wish?

I didn't know.

But driving away from her crumbling house, the propane tank thudding uselessly in the trunk like a body, I knew I couldn't trust Luanne's ravings. Couldn't trust my own, either. I needed something real. And I had nothing.

Chapter 20: The Warning

No sign of the big blue pickup when I hit the junction. I looked right and left, wound down both windows and listened for that sullen, grunting engine. Air and crickets. I felt satisfied with that, and had space to think about something else.

I was getting hungry. I needed to find a place to pull over and plan my next move. A mile or so in the direction of Mingo, I found a spot by what the sign said was a tourist viewing area. Parking for three cars. A hole in the trees revealing a bend in the river. A moss-covered bench. A bin for dogshit.

I turned the engine off. *Unfinished business.* I'd repeated the phrase so often in my mind that it no longer had an echo of dread—it was a starting pistol. I just didn't know which way the race was going to run.

My stomach growled, as loud as that damned Ram had. There must be a bar someplace around here, where I could wash myself, get a beer and a burger. Maybe even find someone who needed propane. I needed fuel for the car too, soon. I grabbed the phone and started Googling—and then it hit me.

My dad is a working man, and Irish too—no way he was sober every day. Was he a regular in a local bar? Classic, desperate detective move. Maybe a sullen barman would tell me everything I needed over a couple of beers and a slipped twenty. Even if it was just the news that my old man was crazy enough to be barred, at least it would help me decide which of the two stories I believed.

It was a long shot, but it was the only shot I had.

Bars near Mingo, WV.

The screen filled with relics of a lost town.

The Blue Parrot Bar & Grill: PER-MANENTLY CLOSED.

The Mountaineer Tap House: PERMANENTLY CLOSED.

Jenny's Roadside Inn: PERMA-NENTLY CLOSED.

It was a digital graveyard of places where people used to gather. But there was one. Just one. The Black Diamond Saloon. No website. No reviews. Just a pin on a map and a single, grainy photo of a low-slung building with a neon sign. My only option.

I started the engine, checked my mirror, and saw a black-and-white patrol car zip past me—he slowed, stopped, put it in reverse and backed into the parking zone ahead. His siren whooped twice.

What the hell is this now?

He left me to wait a minute, then got out, a thickset man with red hair, probably being crucified every day in this climate, and not a guy to mess with. He stopped in front of my car, took a note of the license plate, and then came to my window. His badge said Brody.

"You broke down?"

"No, I'm just parked while I look for a place to eat around here."

"Not local, then?"

"No, I'm down from Ohio."

"Got a license and registration?"

I reached in my purse for my license.

"It's my friend's car—I borrowed it. Don't have the registration documents, but I can give you her name."

"Your name's Erin Callahan?" he said, looking at my document and back at my face.

"Yes."

"Wait here."

He sat in his car for a full minute, just to let me sweat. Then came back.

"You from Lancaster Ohio?"

My throat closed. I nodded.

"We had a call from a Detective Demko, told us he'd lost track of you, thought you'd come to Tug Park. I've just been there, lookin' for your father."

"Listen, Officer Brody—"

"*Chief*," he said, and tapped his insignia.

"Chief Brody?" I asked.

He nodded.

"Seriously? Like *Jaws*?"

He looked at me hard for a second.

"Get out the car."

I sighed and did as he said, just as a growl erupted behind me—and the blue Ram swept past.

"Listen—" I started.

"No, *you* listen. This Demko, up north, he told me to find a Garrett Callahan, and told me you'd be there too. So I've got you. Where's Garrett Callahan?"

"I don't know. I'm looking for him."

"You don't go lookin' for people. We do that. You need to get back to Ohio and report to this Detective Demko. Or I'll book you and take you there myself, and then it'll be harder for me, and for Demko—but *especially* for you."

"Okay, but listen…"

He listened. He'd heard every excuse before— but he went through the motions.

"That truck that just went past? I think that's him. My dad. Garrett Callahan."

Brody looked up the road.

"He's been following me all morning. I keep seeing him."

"You sure it's him?"

"Sure it's Garrett? No… but I'm sure it's the same pickup."

He shot me a cynical look.

"Bet you can't even tell me the plates."

My mouth opened and closed. "No, but it's the

same one every time. He's had—"

"Listen to me."

"—the exhaust done, whatever, and it's louder—"

"*Listen to me!*"

I shut up.

"You're getting back in your car, right now, and heading to Ohio. If you don't, I *will* arrest you. You understand me?"

He handed my license back.

I got in, fuming. One day I'd meet a cop who gave a shit what I had to say.

He took off his hat, revealing a white band where the sun hadn't burned his pale skin raw.

"You go north. Get on US-33 and keep going. Now—before you set off, I need a description of Garrett Callahan. What can you tell me?"

I thought for a moment.

"He's got black eyes. Like a doll's eyes…"

"Get out of the fucking car."

He kept me in the back of his patrol car for an hour

while he called Demko and reported in. Cops must be born with different ears, because I couldn't understand a damn word coming through that radio—but the end result, somehow, was that I wasn't going to be arrested. Just told to get the hell out of the state.

I don't know if that was a *forever* thing, or just this one time, but to seal the deal, I cracked my window as I drove away, and shouted that he was gonna need a bigger badge. Not sure which of us was shaking with anger the most. Maybe me, at the entire goddamn thing. Whatever I'd been closing in on—truth, danger, something—I could feel it slip away. And now I was ordered home, back to square one—trapped in four walls, hounded by the media, waiting for a killer to find me, or Demko to charge me, or Brody to bite me in half.

The road took me north, back through the cramped, crushing woods. The snaking blacktop. The whole time, I was sure I was still being followed. About to be murdered by Garrett in that Ram. And if not? I'd die of hunger first.

"Fuck this," I muttered, and on a rare straightaway, I checked my phone.

The Black Diamond Saloon. Still the last thing I'd mapped. It was in the general direction I was headed—back toward Mingo and the main interstate. All I had to do was make a small detour. Eat.

Maybe ask a couple of innocent questions, and then get out, before I ended up spending the night in jail.

I was so focused on looking for the road sign, I almost missed him: pulled under a tree, half-hidden by shade. The Ram 1500. That dazzling blue. Those custom exhausts—like the open throats of huge animals.

My heart jumped.

I'd just overtaken him.

I looked in the mirror. Nothing. Just the road unspooling wildly behind me, curling into trees and blind bends.

Maybe all of this was a coincidence. Maybe he didn't see me. Maybe I was safe. Maybe—

Shit.

There he was.

And gaining fast.

What the hell had I been thinking? I'd come hunting a killer, and now he was hunting me. I had no plans for this, no end-game. All I could do now was run.

I floored it. The Corolla barely responded—just a thin whine from the engine—and already the sound of the big pickup was drowning it out. The road twisted and writhed like a tortured thing, and on tight corners, I had the advantage. I gained ground in each hairpin, buying myself seconds. But the moment it straightened—even a little—he surged.

A hundred yards behind me. And a corner.

Then seventy. And a bend.

Fifty.

Thirty.

Garrett—if it was Garrett—meant business. But I meant to live.

I was barely braking now. Taking the corners insanely hard. Gripping the wheel like a weapon, no longer checking the mirrors. Every cell in my body was focused on what lay ahead. On escape. On survival. I couldn't outrun him, and I had no idea where any of these roads led. If I took a detour, I could be driving into a dead-end. A farm track bleeding into exposed fields.

The only plan I had left was this: get to the bar. Find safety in crowds.

The turn-off for the Black Diamond was a hundred yards away, and I floored it as it approached, squeezing everything I could out of the tiny, useless engine, holding off braking until the last possible second. I flashed my eyes in the mirror—Jesus, he was barely thirty feet behind, his grill filling my view.

Wait for it. Wait… Just a little more…

At the last second I slammed my foot down on the brakes. The Corolla skidded and slid on the dusty surface, and his truck twisted to avoid hitting me. I yanked the steering wheel left—the propane crashing in the trunk—my car crossing his path with inches to spare… and the big Ram sailed past the turning, buying me minutes.

I'd almost stopped completely during the hard braking, but now I slipped back into low gear and gunned it, opening the distance while the Ram battled to reverse and maneuver.

The road—thank God—wound down and up, blocking the view, hiding me from my pursuer. I looked back, rearview and side mirrors, checking every angle, staying at the highest speed I could. I glanced down at the phone—quarter mile to the Black Diamond.

Made it. I pulled over into the parking lot and stopped. No, this was wrong. It was empty. The light was on over the door, but not a single vehicle. I was exposed here—I started up again, crept around the side of the low, flat-roofed building, and found another spot, away from the road.

I didn't wait to catch my breath, just got out, and ran to the door of the bar, and in.

It was a long, dark room with a sticky floor and the light turned off over the pool table. So much for the safety of crowds: the only other person in the entire establishment was the man behind the bar, another gaunt, stooped figure with a face like a forgotten roadmap.

Is this where they all come from—these pendulous, lost men? Or just where they all end up?

He was polishing a glass with a rag that looked older than he was. He looked up as I walked in, halfway to surprise, trying to avoid hope. It was painful to see.

"Afternoon," he said, his voice sandpaper. "What can I get for ya?"

I sat at the bar, the vinyl of the stool sighing under my weight. Paige's car keys made a loud clatter as I dropped them on the counter.

I panted, my eyes fixed on the doorway, waiting...

"Miss? Get you a drink?"

"Can't drink", I said, still watchful, counting the seconds, knowing that by now the Ram would have passed by.

"Sorry," I said again, finally meeting his eyes. "I'm driving, I can't drink. I'm looking for someone. Garrett Callahan?"

His hope died, replaced by that weary, familiar disappointment. I felt it for him. But I had to carry on. "He's my dad, but we lost touch. He's not in trouble, I'm just—I wanna reconnect. He's an older guy, used to have dark brown hair but he'd probably be gray by now. He'd been a carpenter."

With each extra detail I gave him, any flicker of recognition moved further away.

"Don't know him," he said, speaking absolute truth. "Don't know most folks anymore. They all moved on."

Another dead end. I nodded, slid off the stool, and made to leave.

"Thanks anyway."

"You, uh… you sure you don't want a drink before you go?" he asked, his voice cracking slightly with a need he was trying to hide.

Every instinct for self-preservation screamed at me to walk away. Garrett in the Ram was hunting me. Every dollar I spent was a bullet I might need later. The smart play was to leave. But I looked at his face—at the threadbare shirt, the tremor in his hands, at the profound, crushing loneliness of this empty room. He wasn't just a stranger. He looked how I felt. And I'd done enough walking away.

"Yeah," I said, sitting back down with a sigh. "Yeah, I'll have a beer. Whatever's on tap."

He pulled the draft with a slow, careful precision, like it was a sacred ritual. Set the glass in front of me on a damp coaster. I hid the small roll of cash in my purse as I peeled off one—then another—and told him to keep the change. His relief was so naked it was hard to watch.

The beer was shit. I'd worked in bars—I knew when the lines hadn't been cleaned. It tasted like pipe fluid, but I smiled as I drank, so he could feel it. I was sitting in a ghost bar in a ghost town, with a ghost of who this man used to be, chasing a ghost of a father.

Gravel crunched outside. I looked up. There, through the window, I could see it. A huge, vivid blue pickup. It had stopped outside. I saw it move as the weight of the man inside shifted. Heard the door slam.

The world slowed. I stood. Scanned the room. A green emergency exit sign at the back. Maybe past the barman, and into whatever that back room was—but is that a trap? Maybe there was a cellar I could get into…

No time. The bar door opened.

And he stood there.

Shirtsleeves.

Eddie.

Chapter 21: The Bar

"You fucking bitch," he said, low and deadly as a cobra.

I moved away from the bar, towards a table wrapped around a brass pole, surrounded by stools—I stepped behind it, a barrier between Eddie and me. I realized I still had my drink in my hand, and put it down.

"Whatever this is…" said the barman in a slow, cautious voice.

Eddie ignored him.

"You fucking bitch," he repeated. "You told them about the fight, and the gun."

"Goddamn it, Eddie," I snapped back, the fear making me reckless. "The fight was in a public bar. What did you think was gonna happen?"

"I'm calling the cops," came a trembling voice from behind the bar. I glanced over. He wasn't calling anyone. He was just hiding, crouching. We were on our own.

"And I didn't even know you had a gun, you moron."

A gun? Stop calling him a moron. Be Helen. Submit. Defuse.

I softened my voice, my posture. "Eddie, c'mon, baby. Let's just talk about this. Why would I ever turn you in? You've been nothing but good to—"

He wasn't buying it. He grabbed a stool by one of its legs and hurled it at me. The thing was solid oak, heavy as a dead body. It smashed into the table, the wood splintering with a sound like a gunshot, and as I flinched back, he was already striding towards me, circling the table clockwise. I moved with him, a panicked mirror image, keeping the wrecked furniture between us.

"Eddie, calm down! I didn't say a goddamn thing to the cops!"

"Get out of my place," the barman whimpered from behind the counter.

Helen again.

"Listen to me, Eddie, you're wrong. You..." My eyes darted around. *The door. Too far. The exit sign at the back. Maybe.* He swiped at me over the circular table, his knuckles grazing the air inches from my face. I swung around the table again—I was getting closer to the front door now, maybe I could...

"...you matter to me," I finished, the lie tasting like ash in my mouth.

He stopped. His eyes went wide, not with feeling, but with pure, animal rage at my attempt to play him. *Jesus, he's a big guy.* He looked like he was about to rip the table right out of the floor.

"That shit," he snarled, "doesn't work no more."

And I ran.

I bolted for the front door, a blind, desperate sprint, but he was too close. His fist closed around a handful of my hair and yanked. The world tilted violently. I was over, falling backwards, legs kicking at nothing as he dragged me across the sticky floor. My scalp was on fire. I clawed at his wrist, but his grip was iron. He was dragging me towards the bar, towards all those hard surfaces and the neat pyramid of shattering glass behind it.

"Leave her be!" shouted the barman, finally finding his voice.

Eddie paused his dragging to bellow back at the man, "*Shut the fuck up!*" In that single, split-second of distraction, I twisted, pulled, got one foot under me and tried to stand. He still had my hair, part of my ear, my whole skull locked in the vise of his left hand. A hard jolt snapped my head sideways, my cheek flaring with a white-hot pain. He was still holding on, his left hand tangled in my hair, his right palm lifting to hit me again.

There was no thought. Just instinct. I wrenched my head sideways, felt something tear along my scalp, and ignored the pain. I locked my teeth on the soft flesh of his inner forearm and bit down, sickeningly, until my jaw ached. I heard his teeth grit behind a wild, strangled roar. His flesh was as thick and sour as orange peel in my mouth. I tasted sweat, salt, then the unmistakable metal tang of blood. He let go.

I was up. Scrambling away. Not for the door— that hadn't worked. I shoved him as he staggered back, clutching his arm, and put the round table between us again, my eyes frantically scanning for an escape, for a weapon. Biting had bought me time, but his blood was up now. His blood was on his arm, and now it was on my mouth, my shirt...

Miss Calley. I'm scared.

He lunged again, a wounded bull, hand grasping at me over the table, stretching—missing—and I grabbed the half-empty glass of shitty beer, and smashed it against his head.

I thought it would shatter, like it does in movies. It didn't. It just bounced off him, spilling beer across his head and the floor. He hollered in shock more than pain, buying me a precious second. I turned and ran, not for the door, but for the back of the room, for the darkness.

The fire exit! I'd run right past it.

Trapped. No way out.

Frantic, I scanned. My eyes landed on the pool table, a dark island in the gloom. I reached it, grabbed a solid, heavy eight ball, spun and threw it in a single, desperate, uncoordinated movement. It went wide, smacking into the wall behind him, but it made him flinch, reset his charge. I grabbed another. The solid white cue ball. This one was aimed. He saw it coming and twisted, and it caught him on the hip with a flat slap. He grunted, but kept coming.

Then my hand found the smooth, lacquered wood of a pool cue. I snatched it up and held it out in front of me, a clumsy, two-handed grip, like a flaming torch to keep a tiger at bay. Swung it. Again. A huge whistling arc, stopping him dead, just out of reach.

"Come on, you fucking coward!" I screamed, my voice cracking.

"Leave her alone, man!" came the barman's voice from behind Eddie. Eddie turned, impatient at the distraction, and threw a brutal, short punch. The barman sagged to the floor, loose-limbed, strings cut.

In the moment before Eddie turned his attention back to me, his mistake made, I swung the cue with all my weight behind it. The thick end struck him directly on his ear with a nauseating, percussive thud. A thin line of blood immediately traced its way across his cheek. He swung a wild, clumsy fist at me, but his balance was already gone. His foot slipped in the puddle of beer, and he went down, crumpling on his side. His hand went to his bleeding ear, and he let out a high-pitched sound, a squeal of pure shock and pain.

He lay on his side, his knees drawn up, and I didn't hesitate. I kicked him. Hard. I was aiming for his balls, but I might have gotten him in the asshole, or maybe somewhere between. He made a weirdly girlish cry, and rolled onto his front, groaning, trying to push himself up.

I'd already leaped over him and the unconscious form of the barman, and bolted out the front door into the blinding sunlight.

Shit, my car is all the way around the back!

SHIT, I left the keys on the bar!

Back inside. Eddie was on his hands and knees by now, head still down, shaking. I ran past, snatched the keys from the counter, and gave his head one last, solid kick, directly on the top of his scalp with the toe of my shoe. Then out, out into the heat, into the Corolla. I didn't even try to turn it around. I slammed it into reverse, spun the wheel, and shot backwards along the side of the building, and I didn't stop. Not for traffic. Not for breath. Not for anything.

I swung the wheel, and raced away, just me, the road, and the blood.

I passed signs for US-33 three times before I had the courage to stop. My hands were shaking so much I doubted I could keep going. I climbed out, knelt on the ground, and gasped, mouth open and dripping, sure I would vomit. My legs felt like they wouldn't hold me, and my heart was pounding. Every part of me hurt.

When, after a minute, I realized I wasn't about to throw up from sheer adrenaline, I flopped over on my back in the deep grass on the side of the road, and gazed at the dazzling sky until all I could see was white. The fear of the day oozed out of me, sweated into the soil, and I stayed where I was until I felt wrung out, folded tight again, and packed back inside my own shell.

I drove, found a gas station, filled up, and spent half an hour in the restroom, shitting myself loosely, over and over, and in between, dabbing the blood from my scalp with wet toilet tissue. In the mirror the handprint on my face looked huge—and there was a thick, red welt on my ear and neck, where Eddie's iron fist had held me. I ran cold water on my wrists until my blood cooled, then sat on the toilet and finished two cigarettes, back-to-back, under a no-smoking sign.

I paid for the gas, and two bottles of carbonated water, one of which I drank completely before I'd even made it back to the Corolla. I moved from the gas pump to a parking spot, put my hands on the wheel, laid my head on my hands, and gazed in silence at my feet.

Maybe an hour passed, and then my phone rang—crude and sudden in this stilled, dying place. It was Noah.

My first instinct was to ignore it, to wall off the one decent thing in my life from this new, toxic certainty. He didn't need this. He didn't need the parts of me that drew this kind of darkness, the parts that were stained by decades of secrets. But I answered anyway.

"Hey."

"Hey. You okay?"

"Yeah, I'm good, I'm—no, actually. Went to a

bar, and…"

Whatever explanation that was gonna be, it ran out.

"Nice," he said. "Whereabouts?"

"West Virginia."

"Okay. Didn't expect that. Are… are we okay? I dropped by but Ray said you'd gone, and wouldn't say anything else. And you were quiet after the interview at the church. If I've done something to—"

"No," I said. His voice was so full of genuine concern it felt like a physical blow. "No, it wasn't you. I just… I had to come here."

He paused.

"You coming back?"

"Noah, listen—I haven't told you everything about the school. And Lomax. And Eddie, the guy who hit you."

"That guy's an asshole."

No shit.

"Noah…" I was too tired to think straight. I sat back, regrouped, tried again. "Noah, the cops think my dad's involved. In the shooting. And I think I know where he is. Or I did, anyway. Not sure now."

"Wait, hold on—your dad is involved how?"

"Noah, this is my mess."

"But I can help with messes. I have aprons and cleaning fluids."

A laugh broke loose—dry, bitter. "No, you can't, Noah."

"I can," he insisted, his voice gentle but firm. "I want to. I want to help."

"You don't. Trust me."

"Try me."

I put the phone away from my ear and thought about this for a moment. I needed Noah to be clean. Or rather, I needed to be clean for Noah. But whatever this was, me and him—it couldn't grow in the shadow of Garrett, of Eddie. I had to solve this alone, even though I didn't know how.

But… wait. I thought again. Maybe letting Noah in, letting the smart guy in, letting him help… maybe that was the best way forward?

"Okay, listen. I tracked him down to a place in West Virginia, Tug Fork. But he's not here, and his neighbors say he's gone back up to Lancaster, or somewhere nearby. Just abandoned everything and headed off. Recently. And that kinda…"

"It kinda fits."

"It kinda does."

We sat on that for a moment.

"I'm sorry Erin."

"You didn't do anything wrong."

I'm scared.

I know, Della, but I'm trying. I'm trying.

"But the thing is, unless I find him… I can't trust Lomax to do it. She had me in for questioning, and she made my whole life look like I was in the goddamn Sopranos. And they've arrested people that I know have nothing to do with this. Eddie, the guy who punched you—he's a fucking idiot, but he's not a school shooter. If he was, he'd have…"

Killed me an hour ago.

"Anyway, he's *definitely* not the guy I saw stalking me outside my house. The cops are on the wrong path, and I—I need to get him, Noah. I don't know if he really is the shooter. My dad, I mean. And I'm not going to go after him alone. It's getting too risky. But I need to find him, lead the cops to him, or I'll never be free of this."

"Okay… so…" carefully planning his question, "Let's say he *isn't* the shooter—why did he come back to Lancaster in a hurry?"

"I don't know. Someone down here says he was coming back to keep my mom away from me. Other people though—they said he had *unfinished business.* But maybe that doesn't mean what we think. Maybe it really is just work. Actual business. They said he couldn't find a job down here, because he's got a police record."

"What's his job?"

He didn't ask about the record.

"A carpenter. We used to joke that Mom only married him because he did the same job as Jesus."

"A carpenter," he repeated. No comeback, no laugh. I could hear the gears turning. "Okay. Well, that's something I can look into."

"Look into what? Carpenters in Ohio? How's that going to work?"

"Maybe we can think of a way..." His voice had drifted off. I loved how clever he was. Five steps ahead, and making leaps. He was looking for a way forward, a path through the static. And if he did *his* work, books and study, it would be far from me, far from Eddie, from Garrett. He'd be safe.

Even so...

"This could take forever, Noah."

"You're overestimating how much of a social life I have."

A small, genuine smile touched my lips. "Still..."

"And you're underestimating how much access I have to the library's databases. Anything built, you need town planning records, business permits... I have an archive, remember?"

I was quiet for a long moment, staring at my reflection in the rearview, my mangled, wet hair, my half-red face. I saw a woman who was a mountain of trouble. But maybe she was wrong about this one thing: maybe she wasn't entirely alone.

"Okay," I said softly. "Okay... well... thanks."

"We haven't found him yet. But you say he's not in West Virginia. So come home. I'll do some digging, and let's meet up tomorrow, after I finish work, get a beer and go over the plan. We'll do it together."

He'd said *we*. And he wanted to meet. The wall I'd put up began to crumble. His quick, logical brain. His slow, clever hands, taking hold of a mess and making it clean again. It was a terrible, dangerous idea to let him get any closer to this, but the thought of going back to Lancaster to fight this battle on my own...

"Okay," I said, all fight drained out of me, replaced by a fragile, terrifying spark of hope. "Okay. Together."

I turned onto US-33 in the dying light of the day. For the first time, I felt like I had a direction. I was back on the trail. And this time, I wasn't walking it alone.

Chapter 22: The Hunt

It was gone midnight when I arrived home, jittery from the post-fight rush and too much gas-station coffee. I took a long shower and tended to my head— the torn patch where I'd sacrificed my hair to escape Eddie, the red cheek, and somehow a bleeding graze on my wrist that I didn't even remember feeling. I expected to be awake all night, but fell asleep so fast I had no memory of undressing or turning off the lights.

Noah had messaged me, but I didn't get it until the next morning. Details of the day's plan. I lay in bed, aching to my bones, yet so utterly slack I could have sunk into the mattress and vanished forever. I thought about cancelling on Noah, and spending the day languishing in this beautiful sense of contentment—that I'd defeated the mighty Edward McLure. But my mind began to wake up, even as my body refused, and I hadn't eaten for way too long. So I messaged Noah to confirm, hauled myself out of bed, and made the best out of what yesterday had left of my head.

The roadside diner just off Route 33 was so new that it still had those little pieces of plastic wrap at the corners of the tables, not yet properly pulled off by the team who built it.

Somehow it already managed to smell of old coffee.

Noah was picking diligently at pieces of film when I walked in. He saw me coming, looked like a kid caught cheating at math, and slid along the vinyl seat, away from the scene of his crime.

"Keeping your hands busy?"

"I don't like things left unfinished. Anyway—hi. You came."

"And you brought a list," I replied, nodding at a taupe foolscap folder. He pushed it across the table to me and pointed into the parking lot. "Did you hire a car?"

"No, it belongs to the very angry wife of a man I used to sleep with."

He laughed, then realized I wasn't joking. "Oh." He looked out the window some more.

I hoped one day he'd get used to my occasional, unexpected honesty.

The waitress took our orders, coffee and tea, and a breakfast burrito for me. In the silence that followed, I opened the folder and leafed through the papers.

"Are those Post-its?"

"What's wrong with Post-its?"

"Have you set up a spreadsheet too?"

"I have, as a matter of fact. It's on my laptop in the car."

I held one up. "They're color-coded too."

"I never understood how anybody could manage life without color-coded Post-its."

"Jesus."

He tapped the top sheet of his research, his finger tracing a neat line of ink.

"So, here's the logic. Your dad is a carpenter. And you said he has a criminal record. Now, I figure no one's hiring a guy from two hundred miles away to build a deck or hang a bathroom door. That rules out half of Craigslist."

"Okay."

"So if he's here for work, it has to be a larger project. Something commercial—a new housing development, a warehouse, a big refit. Something that needs a lot of bodies."

I nodded. Hadn't thought of that.

"But it's not gonna be a big firm or unionized crew. Those guys aren't hiring him with a record, and they're definitely not keeping him off the books. So I cut out all the companies who have their values painted on the side of the forklifts."

Okay, this guy is *way* smarter than me. I need to keep him around.

He almost made me value Post-its.

"And that leaves us with… this." He fanned out the papers. There were seventeen names on the list. Seventeen construction sites where a phantom might be hiding.

"Seventeen?" I said, the number feeling both impossibly large and hopefully small. It was a tangible thing, a map of possibilities where before there had been nothing but a suffocating fog.

"That's the shortlist," he said, sipping his tea with a certain irritating air of self-satisfaction. "Seventeen places that are big enough to need the work and maybe shady enough to not care who does it. It might be another dead end. But… well, I've got a few days leave I can take."

"You sure?"

He beamed, like this was going to be an adventure

"Okay," I said, taking a slow breath. I picked up a spoon and stirred my untouched coffee, watching the black liquid swirl. "Okay. Let's go hunting."

Our first stop was a half-finished housing development called "Maple Glen," a name that promised a rustic charm violently at odds with the warscape of mud and machinery we found. A dozen skeletal house frames stood against the sky, wrapped in flapping Tyvek like mummies waiting for a ceremony. We pulled up to the site entrance, unsure if we should just drive in, or find some door to knock on and ask permission.

After a minute sitting in the car, looking around and wondering if this was such a great idea after all, we got out and, rather than stepping through the obvious entry point, we peered through the gap in the wire fence. A man in a hard hat was walking away from us, and Noah hailed him in a friendly, man-of-the-people tone that didn't sell for a second. The guy turned and walked to us as slowly as humanly possible. It was literally impossible for him to look more bored.

"Everything okay?" he asked, in a voice as rough

and flat as tarmac.

"We're looking for someone," I said, breaking out my best smile. "He's a carpenter. Garrett Callahan?"

The guy stepped forward and squinted, first at my face, then at Noah in his corduroys. He held up a hand and walked at a snail's pace to a yellow portacabin, where he disappeared for two minutes. Then he came out again and pointed us out to another man, in a suit ludicrously topped off with a reflective tabard and another hard hat. I could see them making sense of this: two strangers in a clean compact car, wearing clothes that had never seen a speck of drywall dust. We might as well have shown up in IRS windbreakers and matching clipboards.

"I'm the foreman," said the tabard. "How can I help?"

"I'm looking for my dad. He's a carpenter, he works around here, and I'm trying to find him. He's not in trouble—"

"He's got an inheritance," said Noah. *The boy learned fast.*

"His name's Garrett Callahan."

"And he works here, you say?"

"Somewhere around here."

His eyes glazed over as he glanced past me towards an approaching truck. "Never heard of him, lady. We get a lot of guys here."

"Could you check?" Noah asked, leaning across me, his voice polite but firm. "He's her father."

"Yeah, she said. What are you, her husband?"

We hadn't worked out a plan for this, so I shuffled away from Noah, and he shuffled closer, then changed his mind.

"Could you just check?" I repeated. "He's my dad."

"Everyone's got a dad. Look, we're on the clock. I don't know the guy, and I'm not checkin' for every Tom, Dick and Gary. Can't help you."

"Garrett," corrected Noah. There was no response from the foreman's back. He walked away before we could protest, his job done. He'd constructed a perfect wall of pure, unadulterated indifference.

"Okay," Noah called. "Good chat."

As I put the car in reverse, the gravel popping under the tires, he said: "Sixteen to go."

The day dissolved into a montage of wrong turns, dead ends, and cheap coffee. Each new site was a fresh flavor of failure.

At a warehouse construction site in Circleville, a foreman with a face like a clenched fist listened to our story with his arms folded in a picturebook drawing of passive aggression. It turned active the moment we finished.

"You motherfuckers ICE, or somethin'?" he grunted, his hand hovering near the radio on his belt. "Or tax guys?"

We assured him we weren't.

He assured us we should get the fuck off his property anyway, his eyes following us as if he expected us to reach the horizon, turn around, and return with the full weight of federal government.

In Logan, we found a project building a new strip mall, the future home of another vape shop, tan salon, and a discount mattress store. The site manager was a young woman who looked barely old enough to drink, her hard hat perched comically on a head of impeccably styled blond curls. She was sympathetic, her brow furrowed with a performed concern that reminded me of Greevy. She took down my number on a napkin with a perfectly manicured hand, promising to ask around and call me if she heard anything. I felt hopeful, and as I walked away I turned back to thank her again, just in time to see her drop the paper into the mud.

We drove through a maze of back roads to a sprawling, high-end housing development where every construction looked identical—a beige, unfinished monument to beige, unfinished aspiration. This time the union rep was furious at the very idea of Garrett. He gave us a ten-minute lecture on the importance of certified labor, the evils of right-to-work states, and when we mentioned the words "off the books," he looked at us like we were suggesting opening up a heroin outlet next to a high-school.

At an old factory, undergoing renovation into apartments for people who mostly lived out of state, the crew kept their voices muffled behind dust masks, accents carefully shielded, eyes blank with suspicion. We were turned away from a new motel build by a security guard who seemed genuinely thrilled at the prospect of a physical confrontation, like it was the only reason he'd taken the job. One site had been abandoned completely—no workers, no machinery, no tarps or portable toilets. The half-finished structures already being reclaimed by weeds, a developer's sign swinging mournfully on a single hinge.

Failure after failure. Refusal. Denial. Indifference. Suspicion. Each dead end was another small paper cut, slowly bleeding the hope out of me, leaving behind a cold, pragmatic resolve. This was work. This was what it took.

I'd expected this to take two days, maybe three. But most of the sites were clustered close together in a ring around the city, and most of the conversations ended before they even began. By late afternoon we were at number fourteen on Noah's list. We hadn't stopped for lunch, just a quick burger in the car and a bathroom stop at a service station.

Number fourteen was further out. It sat down a long gravel track, off a two-lane highway, miles from the nearest homes—a distribution center being churned into existence in the middle of nowhere. To me, it looked just like the others, but on a huge scale—a vast steel box, a sea of mud, pickup trucks scattered at odd angles, like dropped toys. The only difference was security—the site felt watchful. The fence didn't just keep people out—it kept something in. Even the barbed wire looked angry. The entrance was sealed with a heavy sliding gate, padlocked from the inside. There was no traditionally unfriendly foreman to tell us to fuck off. There was no one to talk to at all.

We drove around the perimeter, as far as the road would take us, and saw almost nothing remotely human. We pulled off half a mile down, under a tangle of trees where the gravel faded back to dirt. Every couple of minutes, the tap of a seed or a leaf falling on the roof.

I told Noah: "This feels right."

"Yeah? Why?"

"It's... I don't know. There's nothing here. Nobody to talk to. No way in. It just...it feels like my dad."

Noah nodded, his eyes scanning the site. We were in a car a hundred yards from the fence, but still spoke in low voices, like we were afraid of being overheard.

"Can you imagine working there?" he asked.

"It's like a cage."

"At least they're outdoors," I said. "Sounds better than being in a library back room eight hours a day."

"Hey, I love my job! I can't imagine these guys love theirs. They take a job like this because they have to. They probably can't get another because they're undocumented. Can't get union help because the union doesn't want shit from ICE. Can't get a pay rise because the boss knows they're powerless. Can't even get off the site, except to visit that Burger King for a toilet break. I can't imagine anything worse than being trapped like that."

The words hung in the air between us.

"Sometimes you remind me of my mom."

He looked at me. "Well, I can't hear that too many times."

"I mean—you seem to have this idea that if you work in an office, you love your job and have choices. But if you work with your hands…"

"That's not how I meant it."

I looked out the window again. Maybe he wasn't so smart after all.

"We're all trapped a bit," I said, quietly.

He nodded. Took a moment. Let it sink in.

"Yeah, I'm sure that's true. I guess I'm just lucky. I like my job."

"I don't," I said. "I mean—I do, but it's not what I wanted. I wanted to be a teacher, a proper teacher. I love the kids. *Loved* them." I drew a deep breath, oddly cleansing. I was talking about them. "I loved them all, but I was just passing out crayons and wiping noses. It's not what I wanted."

He had a gift for letting you just finish a thought.

"Truth is, I fucked up. I had to take a year out of school, because of family shit. And I never got back on board. Never caught up. So now I'm stuck as a paraprofessional. Trapped."

We looked at each other again. I felt a little mended, but he still looked a little hurt. "You're not really like my mom," I said, and then realized I was telling him the truth—he's nothing like her. No way she'd have tried to understand.

"Point made," he said. "Everyone feels trapped, and nobody likes it."

I looked back at the building site.

"I know a goat in Tug Fork that would disagree."

"What?"

"Never mind."

We sat and watched, even though there was nothing to see. Just the sounds of power tools inside that warehouse, of shouted jokes in English and Spanish, drifting on the hot air.

"What are we even looking for?" Noah asked finally. "I have no idea what he looks like."

"I'm not sure I do either," I admitted. "Cops took him when I was fifteen. The only photo I've got is from before then, and it's blurry. He'd be... fifty-five now? Sixty? I don't even know his real age. My mom was always vague on the details."

"Can I see the photo?"

I kept a copy on my phone, scrolled way down to find it, and handed it over. Noah pinched in to look at the face.

"I can't make much out."

"Might not matter," I said, taking the phone back. "A man can change a lot in eighteen years. And anyway, I'm looking for the guy I saw outside my house. That's him now. He's older, his hair's going gray, he's fatter."

We sat and stared. No wonder cops went mad, if stake-outs were like this.

"I need to use the bathroom," Noah said, stretching his arms. "There's a Burger King about a half mile back. I'll be quick."

"Get me a coke," I said, my eyes still glued to the site.

He was gone for less than ten minutes. I barely noticed. I was lost in the rhythm of the work site, the slow dance of men and machinery—they'd make themselves visible occasionally, each one too old or too young, too dark or too pale. I didn't see Noah coming back until he was wrenching open the passenger door, his face ashen, his breath coming in ragged gasps.

"Go," he panted, fumbling with his seatbelt. "Go, now."

"What? What happened?"

"Some guy," he said, his voice shaking. "Big guy in the bathroom. He'd followed me, he grabbed me, got right in my face, told me to fuck off out of town and stop asking questions."

Noah wasn't a fighter. He wasn't built for this. My jaw set hard. "What did he look like?"

"I don't know! Big guy. Construction worker."

"Gray hair?"

He met my stare.

"Yes."

I turned the wheel, one way, then the other, thinking...

"He scared the shit out of me, Erin. Let's just go."

I nodded, turned the wheel away from wherever the guy was, somewhere along that road. I slammed the car into drive, my heart hammering, and we sped away, back down the gravel track and onto the main road. The road took a bend, and Noah was breathing easier, but as soon as the construction site had dropped from view, I pulled a sharp U-turn, tires squealing on the hot asphalt, and headed straight back.

"What are you doing?" Noah yelped, grabbing the dashboard.

"If that's my dad," I said, my voice tight with a strange, predatory calm. "If he's come from the site, then he has to go back this way. I need to see him, make sure it's him."

"Erin, no, that's a fucking a terrible idea—"

But it was too late. I pulled onto the shoulder, killing the engine, my eyes fixed on the road ahead.

"That's the one," Noah said, sinking lower in his seat. "Yeah. That's him."

He was halfway between us and the Burger King, still more than a hundred yards from me, a heat-haze shimmering on the road. He looked... familiar. The shape of him. The way he walked, his head down against the sun. Dark hair with gray. Pale skin. Heavy set. It could be him, maybe. The man from outside my house. It could be Garrett.

The thought sent a jolt through me, raw and electric. Before Noah could stop me, I was out of the car, my feet hitting the asphalt.

"Garrett!" I screamed, my voice cracking. "Garrett Callahan!"

I started running towards him, a wild mix of fear and fury propelling me forward. He stopped, looked up, then glanced around, bewildered. I closed the distance, my heart pounding in my ears, and then, ten feet away from him, my ice-cold certainty melted in the heat. I stopped, rigid, in his path.

He looked at me, and to my astonishment, he was more frightened than I was. His eyes were wide, panicked, and he stood in a defensive posture, one foot forward, one hand out. Rock solid.

"I haven't got any money," he said, his voice shaking.

"What?"

"My wallet, it's back at work. I just came to use the john."

"I don't want *money*."

"What *do* you want?" he said, relaxing his stance

a little.

"I'm looking for my father," I stammered.

"What?"

"My father. I'm looking for him. Are you... are you him?"

He glanced around, as if expecting to be ambushed by cameras or cops. "What the hell is this? Who sent you?"

I heard Noah catching me up, standing behind me. The guy's eyes shifted from one to the other, and I could see him weighing who to fight first.

"Are you Garrett Callahan?" I yelled, the frustration and disappointment making my voice sharp.

"My name's Blake Welton!" he yelled back, ludicrously loud from ten paces. "Who the fuck are you?"

"I'm..." The name died on my lips. Blake Welton. Not Garrett Callahan.

I threw my hands up and turned to Noah. Another dead end. All that frenzy, all that hope, all that fear... it all drained out of me, leaving me weak and immobile on the side of a dusty road.

Noah stepped forward. "I think there's been a mistake," he told the guy. "We're looking for her father."

"Jesus, kid! I thought you were the IRS or something."

This wasn't my father. This wasn't a killer. This was just another working man, trying to get by.

"Sorry I grabbed you in the john, buddy. I saw you two watchin' me all mornin'. Thought you were come for my back-taxes."

We sat in the car, the engine off, the air thick with the smell of failure and anticlimax. I was panting, the adrenaline leaving a bitter taste in my mouth. Noah was staring straight ahead, his knuckles white as he gripped the taupe folder on his lap.

"Well," I said finally, the words catching in my throat. "That was a bust."

Noah turned to me, a strange look on his face. "On the bright side," he said, his voice still a little shaky, "I don't think I'll need the toilet again for at least a week."

A laugh escaped me, a short, sharp bark that was half sob. The tension shattered, and suddenly we were both laughing, a hysterical, breathless laughter that filled the small car. We were laughing because we were alive, because we were idiots, because the whole world was insane.

We were still catching our breath when my phone rang. The screen showed Ray Garcia's name. A wave of relief washed over me. A normal person. A link to the real world.

"Hey, Ray," I said, a smile still in my voice.

"Erin? You need to come home," he said, and the smile vanished from my face. His voice was tight, urgent. "Come home right now. There's been a break-in at your place. And Erin… sorry, but Eddie's out on bail."

You don't say.

Chapter 23: The Homecoming

Ray spent half an hour apologizing. He'd been in his garden when he heard a banging on my front door and assumed it was the media again. He told Connie to call the cops, and clambered over the fence, only to walk straight into a gym body, parked next to a giant pickup, screaming abuse at my house.

Ray told him to get lost.

Eddie told Ray to fuck off, and shoved him.

"He's a big guy, Erin."

"I know that, Ray, it's not your fault."

"He said he'd kick the shit out of me, and I believed him. I'm so sorry."

In the end, Ray told Eddie I'd gone to Tug Fork. I probably would have too, if I wasn't standing next to a fully loaded pool table.

"You didn't do anything wrong," I told Ray, recycling the bullshit everybody had sold to me.

My first instinct, a sharp, selfish pang, was that I needed to get home. But I couldn't. Not yet. Noah was still with me, a silent passenger in a borrowed car. His own was still miles away in long-term parking. He'd followed me down this rabbit hole—I couldn't just leave him at the bottom.

He let me be silent during the drive back towards Lancaster, as I turned things over in my head and came to a decision.

"First thing," I said, my voice steadier than I felt, "I need to get you back to your car."

"No way," he said. "You know as well as I do that this isn't some random smash-and-grab. This is your dad. Or Eddie again. Or both."

"I'm not dragging you into this shit."

"I'm already in it."

I glanced over at him. He looked scared—I probably did too—but he went on, making his case.

"I know I was useless back there, but I'm not just leaving it all up to you. After all this? You've been through enough. The shooting, your dad, that creep watching you, the media. And your mom sounds like a challenge. And the goat. I love that you've— it's great that you've got chutzpah, but you can't do everything alone. And I've come this far, and—"

"The cops will be there."

"—*oh, thank Christ*, because I was going to be

useless at your home too."

We picked up his sad little car, looking like a lost puppy in the middle of the empty lot, and set off in convoy. God knows what route he thought I was taking, but when we pulled up on a street he'd never visited before, I could see his bewildered face in my rearview mirror. I put on fresh make-up, tied my hair in a bun, and walked back to him. He cracked the window.

"Do you wear glasses?"

"Sometimes," he said. "Just for reading."

"Perfect. Put them on. And your jacket. Bring the laptop and all the papers. And back me up here."

He stood two paces behind me in his corduroy, glasses and moustache, bolt upright and banjaxed. I rang the bell. I didn't know how this would go. I just knew it had to.

Ty answered, pale as a haunted moon. He had a red swelling under his left eye.

"Oh shit, no," he whispered, a prayer and a plea. "Not again, Jesus."

"Good afternoon, Mr. Holcomb", I said, in voice calibrated to reach Paige way back in the house. "I'm returning the car. I just want to thank you on behalf—"

A thundercloud swarmed up the hallway behind him. This was it. Showtime.

"Ah," I said, delighted, with a box-fresh smile, my arms spread in welcome. "Mrs. Holcomb! Hello again."

Her eyes narrowed. This didn't add up at all.

"I just wanted to return your car, and thank you so much for the loan. You have no idea how much it helped."

She looked at Ty, looked at me, looked at whoever the hell was behind me.

Stay strong, buddy, we can do this.

"Oh, you haven't met Noah. Noah Rafferty, this is Paige Holcomb. She's the one who loaned us the car. Noah is our school librarian. He's been out with me today, visiting with the families, coordinating support."

Noah made a noise like a trapped rabbit and held out his hand. He was perfect for this. She turned to Ty, who appeared to have evaporated into the background. "Go inside," she said, like you'd talk to a scolded dog.

"Fuck, honey," she said as she turned back to me, all the fight gone. "I had you wrong." The presence of this mild-mannered, bespectacled man had done what all my bluffs and bullshit couldn't: it had made my lie the truth. No mistress, no matter how bold, shows up with her own nerdy librarian.

"I understand," I said, leaning in conspiratorially, "I dated one like that once. Never again."

She looked me in the eye, a moment of raw, unvarnished truth passing between us. "I'm stuck with mine."

I gave a wry nod. "So sorry for your troubles." I touched my cheek, light and approving, mirroring the same spot on Tyler.

"Oh, he had it coming," she said.

I gave a sisterly shrug. I thought she was going to embrace me.

"Well... thank you again for the car."

"You take care of yourself, you hear me?"

"You too," I said. And I meant it.

As Noah started the engine, he turned to me, his face a perfect mask of bewilderment.

"What the fuck was all that about?"

I settled into the passenger seat, a wave of profound, exhausted satisfaction washing over me. "We did the Lord's work today, Noah," I said. "We saved a terrible marriage. Or at the very least, we saved somebody from getting their face smashed in."

The small triumph with Paige didn't survive the drive. Every headlight in my rearview felt like a pursuit. I gripped my knees, my knuckles white, turning onto East 6th. Dread sat heavy in my gut. I was certain the sanctuary I was being driven toward was already gone.

Ray Garcia was waiting on my porch, his solid presence a small island of calm in a rising sea of chaos. Across the street: a guy with a camera on a folding chair, who sat up and got to work when I arrived.

I couldn't give a shit. My front door hung open, the frame splintered, the wood around the lock a jagged wound. "Ah, fuck me," I said at the violation. But as I stepped inside, my fear gave way to a strange, disorienting confusion.

I'd braced myself for a scene of cinematic bedlam: overturned drawers, smashed pictures, the guts of the sofa spilling onto the floor. But there was nothing. No worse than it had been after the Ohio PD and I scrubbed it within an inch of its life. If it weren't for the savaged doorframe, I might not have even known anyone had been here. The television was still on its stand. The prints on the walls were straight. The pile of books on the coffee table was undisturbed. Nothing of value seemed to be gone. It was quiet. It was untouched.

This wasn't a burglary. It certainly wasn't a ransacking. The room looked so neat I half-expected to offer scones.

Ray and Noah lingered awkwardly in the hallway, unsure if they were guests or witnesses.

"I don't get it," I said.

A figure stepped into the doorway behind them, in the familiar blue and white of the Lancaster PD. A uniformed officer, and my stomach clenched.

Kessler.

Oh perfect.

He nodded at Ray, his eyes lingering on Noah with a dismissive curiosity, then settled on me. He walked into my lounge, all swagger and cheap authority.

"We meet again."

"My lucky day," I said, keeping distance between us as he wandered around the room.

"Dispatch told me you'd been burgled. It doesn't look like it. You sure?"

Ray, near the entrance, said, "You seen the door-frame, man?"

They went to look. Noah wandered over to me. "You okay?"

"I'm fine. Just tired."

Mostly I wanted to be alone with this. He said: "I've… I've got work in the morning—and three layers of flop-sweat to wash off."

"Thanks, Noah. I'm fine. I'll call you."

"You'd better."

Ray said his goodbyes to Noah, and told me he was heading home too, but would be back later to patch the door until I could get it fixed properly.

Kessler watched them leave. "And then there were two."

He started moving around the room with a note-book and a pen, looking at my books and pictures. He hadn't written a damn thing down.

"Most girls offer me a drink," he said, his back to me.

"Would you like a drink, Officer Kessler?" I asked, the words automatic, empty.

He turned to look at me.

"I'm good."

He went upstairs, came back, waggled my broken door on its hinge, and then paused in the entrance to the lounge, looking right at me. I had my back to the kitchen counter. We stood silently. I couldn't even hear traffic noises. I wondered how quickly I could get over my back fence.

"Nice kid," said Kessler. "Scrawny though. Is that the one who got into the fight with Eddie McLure?"

"That's him."

"He lost."

Yeah, but I won, I thought, but said nothing. He took one more step into the room. He hadn't taken his cap off this time. He looked around my walls and books.

"Looks like you've got quite a collection."

"I like reading."

"I meant men."

My mouth was too dry to reply.

"There's Eddie. That guy, the mechanic who got shot at. Ray *Garthia*. And now this little boy scout. You work your way through a lot."

"That's none of your business."

"You sure he's your type, Erin?"

"That's none of your business," I repeated, but my voice was quieter now.

He stepped forward again and put his hat on the arm of my sofa.

"From what I can tell, you like the bad boys."

"What the hell do you know?"

His gaze dropped to my feet, then traveled with excruciating slowness up my body, logging every detail. "Oh, I do my research. I've seen you, you know. On the news. You were all over my Facebook, in that hot little number, day after the shooting. Coming home in other clothes... Looked pretty good both ways, darlin'."

My hand reached around for something on the kitchen counter, anything.

"And now this burglary."

I'd cleaned it all away—*Shhhhhit.*

"Maybe you need a real man to take care of you."

Ray had gone home—*Would he hear if I screamed?*

"You owe me a drink. C'mon. I came out to your house, what, three times now? Come out for a drink with me tonight. Wear that thing again, that slutty little one from the news. Bet you've still got it. Dress like that again, and I might even send you home dressed different."

"Fuck off, Kessler."

His smile vanished. "What did you say to me?"

My voice had trembled the first time I said it, so I made sure this time, every word clicking like a safety catch.

"I said. *Fuck. Off.*"

"You think you can talk to a cop like that, you little bitch?"

I met his eye, a strange, exhilarating power surging through me. "That's the difference between a slut and a bitch, Kessler. A slut sleeps with whoever she wants to. She's only a bitch when she doesn't want to sleep with *you!*"

For a second, a long, terrifying second, I thought he was going to hit me. His hand twitched. His face reddened. He inched forward, his shadow falling over me—

"Officer Kessler," said a voice like ice from the door. "Out. Now."

Lomax stepped into the room. He looked around with pure venom, grabbed his hat, and pushed out into the street. I found myself breathing hard. I wiped my palms on my jeans. Lomax didn't say anything. She didn't need to. She just watched me, a look of profound, weary understanding on her face. Sympathy. Recognition. A story we'd heard a thousand times.

"I didn't know he'd be here," she said, quietly.

I nodded, getting my breath.

"Did he do that to the door?"

"No. I've been burgled."

She frowned, blinked, and looked around. "You sure?"

"He said he was the attending officer. Didn't you know? Isn't that why you're here?"

"I'm Major Crimes. We don't get informed about break-ins. I came here to yell at you," she explained in an emotionless voice.

I stood up straight again. "Fuck you! Yell at me for what?"

"For leaving the state without telling me. For running off on your own when there's a man maybe trying to kill you. We had no idea where you were."

A bitter laugh escaped me. "You want to know why I left? Because of *him!*" I pointed towards Kessler, out on the sidewalk. "Because of the two useless dipshits you sent when my dad was watching me from outside my house, who thought I was crazy. Because you two interrogated me like I was the goddamn mafia. Because you arrested Eddie when you should have been looking for my father. And then let him go! And Garrett is still out there, Lomax, and nobody is doing a goddamn thing about it. So yeah. I stepped up."

She didn't argue. She just nodded, letting me vent, her expression unreadable. "Erin, what were you going to do if you found him? He's an armed killer."

"I know that!" I shouted, but she was right. I had no plan when it turned out to be Eddie either. Barely made it out.

I sat on my sofa.

"But he didn't kill me when he had the chance in the school," I said in a tired voice. "No reason for him to kill me if I find him now."

"You're talking about him like he's sane. Like he makes sane choices. Erin, he killed seventeen people. He's not sane. You can't catch him on your own. He won't let you. And I won't let you. Let me do my job."

The truth of her words sunk in. I had been running on pure adrenaline and fear, but she was right. I was out of my depth, chasing a ghost in a nightmare. I leaned back on the sofa, arms up, legs out, drained by carrying the weight of the last few days.

"Didn't you tell me once that there would be counseling?"

She nodded. "I did, yeah. But—limited resource, dozens of families. I don't know the details, but I'd guess you're on a list."

"Meantime, I have to just go crazy on my own?"

She sat next to me in one of her long, cushioned silences. I could see her from the corner of my eye, clicking pieces in her head, testing if they fit, pulling them apart and reassembling them until she found the order that she thought would work. We both stared ahead.

"My dad left when I was kid," she told me, "And I haven't seen him since. My mom died too. But that was later."

She was trying, I could tell, but this wasn't her way. She spoke like she was delivering a report into a cold case she'd filed away many years ago. I tried to find the right response, before she felt forced to make eye contact or hug me.

"We all fight our fights."

"Yep."

"We all have our armor."

"Yep." Her sleeve had ridden up, and the tattoo peeked out. She adjusted her clothes to hide it.

"I can't keep calling you Lomax."

"I'm Gabrielle. Gabi."

I nodded. "Are all families as fucked-up as this?"

"No. But enough." She took a deep breath through her nose, and Gabi turned back into Lomax. Her posture straightened, her voice lost its softer edge, and she could look at me again. "You're sure this was a burglary, and not just a break-in?" she asked, her eyes already scanning the room with a new, professional intensity.

"What's the difference?"

"Burglary means something's missing."

"The only valuable things I've got are my phone and my car," I said. "And you already stole those."

"Actually..." She reached into her bag and pulled out a crinkled evidence envelope. Inside was my phone. "I came to give this back too. And to tell you—you can pick up your car. The school's cleared. It's over."

I looked at her.

"Well—*that* part's over," she said.

"Now we just have to find the killer."

"There's no *we* here, Erin."

"And solve the burglary," I added, looking around the room. *Anything taken?* TV. Knife block. Books. Cheap prints. Everything in its place. Nothing disturbed—until my eyes snagged on the yellow dresser. There was a void there. A blankness that screamed at me. My heart started a low, heavy drumbeat I could feel in my throat.

"What...?" Lomax pressed, noticing my distraction.

I didn't answer. I walked slowly toward the dresser, my feet feeling like lead. It was usually cluttered with junk—ticket stubs, a tube of lip balm, loose change. But now, after all that cleaning, only one thing was supposed to remain. Instead, a rectangle in a layer of dust. A perfect absence.

"The photo," I whispered, my throat tight. I pointed a trembling finger at the spot. "There was a photo. Right there."

Lomax stepped beside me. She shone the small torch from her keychain on the dresser, then looked behind it, under it. Nothing. She straightened up and turned to me, her professional mask cracking just a little. The same impossible question hung in the air between us.

"So," she said, her voice haunted. "A burglar breaks in, ignores everything of value, and steals one thing." She held my gaze, forcing me to the conclusion. "What was the photo of, Erin?"

I had to swallow before I could speak.

"Him," I said. "It was the only photo of my dad."

Chapter 24: The Cost

I spent the day with my mind spinning on a two-pronged spike. Theory one: my dad had been outside my home, watching until the press vanished, and then forced the door. The idea of him lurking in the undergrowth was, somehow, the most comforting option. The other was that he was perched a thousand yards away with a high-powered scope, just waiting.

Theory two was Lomax's, though she'd offered it with no real conviction: that Eddie McLure, newly out on bail, had come for a social call, found me gone, and taken the one thing he knew I valued out of pure spite. Maybe. The timeline made no sense to me—but I knew he was out cold in West Virginia. Lomax didn't. Even so, it was possible. He knew it was the only photo I had.

But he didn't know it was the only photo that existed. And he'd been seen by Ray, when he bullied my West Virginia location out of him. Made no sense that he'd come back to break in before chasing me down.

So my gut, and I suspected Lomax's too, landed on my father. Stealing the photo in the desperate, flawed belief it would make him harder to trace.

I emailed Lomax the blurry copy from my phone before she left. Then the day became a void. I pulled the drapes, and dragged the dresser against the busted front door, hoping it would keep murderers out until Ray got a chance to come around and fix it. It killed ten minutes. By the time I'd thrown away the lunch I was too scared to eat, the silence was so loud I had to get out.

I put on old sneakers and a hoodie and peeked through kitchen window. No press, no smirking neighbors, no lurking killers. I hopped the fence, cut through Ray's yard, pulled up my hood, and walked.

No killers or cops at the school either. Just regular people at the hardest moment they would ever know, holding each other in small groups. There had been thousands, tens of thousands right after the event, a huge outpouring. But now? Just that narrow band—the ones directly affected, but keeping it together enough to go outside, and help hold one another up. A couple in wealthy clothes, soft tweeds and cashmeres, impossibly tight together, learning in real-time that all the money in the world can't do a thing. A mother on her knees by the sea of flowers, her eyes locked in a thousand-yard stare. Some had already found a way to carry on, parents and grandparents murmuring in quiet reminiscence. Others looked so lost they'd never feel again, wandering through the patchwork of grief, finding messages on soft toys, and gently touching names on hand-lettered signs.

An autumnal air of infinite sadness, cast loose in May.

My car had sat behind all of this for days, hidden away in the school parking lot, behind a police cordon and a polite little sign asking *No Media Past This Point*. The tape was gone now, but the flowers were still coming. Lancaster couldn't help itself—roses for grief, balloons for guilt, teddy bears for show.

This was going to be hell. The media might have forgotten my massacre after-party, but the parents wouldn't have. These people had lost their kids, for Christ's sake. I had too—eight of them in my own classroom, right in front of me. But it's not the same.

They keep telling you that. *It's not the same.*

It felt the same.

Even so, I was primed to be meek. Apologetic. Culpable. Whatever words were said, whatever glares I endured, however raw and furious these people were about to be, there was no way I was going to fight back. I had no right.

But when someone stepped out of the grieving crowd to confront me, it wasn't a parent at all—not one I immediately recognized. Blonde, brittle. Skin like paper left in the sun too long.

"You," she said.

Oh, my creeping Jesus.

"Paige…"

"They called me from West Virginia!"

Heads turned.

"You lying fucking *WHORE!*"

Oh my God.

"Wait, Paige…" Her arm swung out to the side, and I started to duck. She connected—a crack of light, and my head and teeth rang like a bell. An involuntary, guttural noise—*nnnng*—came half from my nose and half from my throat, and then her hands were in my hair, yanking and dragging me.

"That's my husband, you *bitch.*"

My head was down, and I grabbed wildly at her wrists. All I could see were feet—hers kicking at me, others gathering around to pull us apart. When I came free, strands of my hair still in her fist, I saw Mikayla Jennings's dad, in black, pulling her away. Another woman tried to soothe her.

Nobody came to help me. They were too busy getting their phones out, too busy filming.

People are always filming.

"I hope you *rot*," Paige shouted, as they dragged her back through the crowd. "I hope God sees what you are!"

I didn't remember falling, but I stood, my palms scuffed across the concrete, torn and bloody. My face ached down to my jawline, and I was sure my scalp was bleeding again, but didn't want to touch it. Not in front of them.

Somebody said, "Girl, she destroyed you."

Only on the outside. Inside, I'd been wrecked for years.

I tried to walk away with dignity, and made it through the gates, but by the time I got to my car I was sprinting.

My hands were shaking so violently I could barely find the ignition. On the first try, I dropped the key between the seats. On the second, my foot slipped off the clutch, stalling with a lurching crunch. Third, it caught, and the tears I'd been holding back finally broke free.

And I got the hell out of there.

I parked up on the roadside halfway home and beat my ripped hands on the wheel until it felt like it was gonna break off.

Then I had to stop. After all, let's be realistic: my mechanic's wife wanted to kill me, and even if I made it past her, the poor guy was under sedation.

I let myself breathe, just sit and breathe.

And I thought Eddie could throw a punch.

This was getting re-goddamn-diculous now.

I risked a glance in the rearview mirror. Christ. The skin around my eye was already puffing up, angry and hot, darkening by the second. I touched it gently, wincing. Right now, it was just the *promise* of a bruise—a sincere guarantee that I'd be a whole galaxy of ugly by morning. Another goddamn headline I'd have to wear all over my face.

I checked my watch—yep. By now, the Paige vs. Erin clips would be on social media, and the whole vicious cycle would be kicking off again. Round Two.

I had to get supplies and bunker down. Especially if I needed to stay safe from my crazy dad, like Lomax had warned me.

I reached into my purse and checked how much cash I had left. An absolute wasteland. And by now my bank would be empty again, the mortgage payment sweeping it clean. Nobody could ever mistake me for a careful shopper, but this time I had to perform some kind of miracle.

I made a mental list of the absolute necessities on my way to Kroger. No beer. No cigarettes. Don't even walk near the Jack Daniel's—the memory alone might make me puke.

I picked up the cheapest, most uncomfortable possible toilet paper. Dried pasta with short use-by dates, and crappy white bread I could freeze. Peanut butter, a half dozen cans of beans, and store-brand coffee. A little jolt of joy and camaraderie when I spotted special offer apples, bruised enough to be cheap.

I was loading bags into the back seat when I saw him, over the road, filming me. Some skinny teenager.

Not even thirty minutes since the school, and already I was a target again. Probably trending again, too. They move that fast. They eat that fast.

I had nothing to lose now.

"Hey," I yelled across the road to him.

He stood still, phone held high.

"Go to hell, you bloodsucker!"

Shameless. He just carried on like I wasn't a person.

"You think this is funny? You think dead kids is funny?"

I saw red. *Della Morrison*. Wasn't even thinking when I grabbed the first can of beans and hurled it at him.

"You sick piece of shit!"

Another can. Then the peanut butter in its plastic tub—it bounced, high and wide, close enough to make him flinch. I was getting good at this, so I reached into the bag and pulled out the coffee. Big jar. Glass.

This one would break. This one had consequences for me too, and I really didn't want to do it, but I'd started now, so…

He turned and calmly walked away.

He'd gotten what he needed. Even the vampires were abandoning me now.

God, if Noah could see this… He'd check my face was still attached, then say something smart and dumb, or dumb but smart, that would snap me right out of it. I could almost hear his voice as I crouched to pick up the dented cans, watched by two women with strollers. "Yet another public unraveling from the undisputed champion."

At least I didn't cry. I couldn't risk adding more liquid behind the crumbling dam I had built. I just picked up the food and drove to Cherry Street. By the time I'd got through Ray's yard and scrambled over the back fence with the bags, I was sweating, my hair stuck to my face—and I still had to bash the dents out of the beans so my shitty can opener would grip them.

I held one against the counter and beat it with a saucepan, trying to flatten the warped edge into something like a circle.

Bang.

I barely even knew Paige.

Bang.

Fucked her husband. Lied to her face. Took her car.

Bang!

If I could ruin her life like that, she had every right to ruin mine.

Bang!

What the hell was I going to do? I was already borderline unemployable. After this, I doubted I could get a job anywhere. Not one with dental insurance.

Bang! Bang!

I couldn't pay any more bills. Couldn't show my face at school, online, even at Kroger.

Bang! Bang! Bang! BANG!

I brought the saucepan down one last time with all my weight behind it. The tin split. Syrup and beans sprayed my shirt and counter. I stood there, panting, saucepan still in hand, staring at the wreck of my own pathetic dinner. The rage was gone, replaced by a hollow, aching emptiness.

That's when the tap came at the back door.

Ray saw my eye, and his smile faltered for just a moment before he forced it back into place. I hadn't even looked at it since I got home. I didn't care. The throb from my cheekbone barely touched the pain inside me.

"Hey, Erin, how you doing? Can you help me out?"

He was holding a large baking dish with a towel over it.

"Connie made too much lasagna, and Ray Junior is at his girlfriend's for the weekend—we're never gonna eat all this."

I took the dish from him. It was heavy, home-made, and no way they cooked it today. It was still slightly frozen on the bottom. I felt my face crumble.

"Thank you, Ray."

He nodded, started to leave, then stopped and laid his hand on mine.

"Drop off the dish when you're feeling—whenever. Just whenever."

Baby's Breath

Chapter 25: The Date

There wasn't enough concealer in the world to hide this. By morning, my eye had expanded the rainbow into a palette of green, brown and lurid purple. I stood at the bathroom mirror, gently poking my swollen cheekbone, replaying it all. That tightrope walk with Paige, Ty, and Noah— God, it had felt solid. I had her convinced—and then Officer fucking Jaws from West Virginia had to step in, had to tell Paige the whole damn story. Just my dumb luck to walk into her in the exact location where the town's biggest, most judgmental crowd was gathered to watch the rest of the circus. Caught on camera, of course—one more little gift for the newsroom ghouls. One more public humiliation I'd have to cope with.

I realized I'd begun prodding the eye harder and harder, and made myself stop.

Christ, I wonder what Tyler's eye looks like. At least I got away. He's stuck there.

I upended my entire makeup bag onto the floor in the bathroom, and gazed at it. I'm a thirty-three-

year-old woman, and this is what I have to show
for it: a dried-out mascara, a half-used lipstick, and
a collection of samples I'd pilfered from magazines.
I experimented with them, but it was like trying to
cover the Valentine's Day Massacre with a glitter pen.

I had an idea. Rooting through the back of my
yellow dresser, amongst the single socks and old
receipts, I found it: a small, cheap palette of green
eyeshadow I'd bought years ago for a St. Patrick's
Day party I had tried to block out. I popped the
cracked lid and looked at it—an aggressively ugly
blob, with an artificial eyelash stuck to the surface. I
picked it off and flicked it away. Why bother keeping
the place clean? It was unofficially hosting murderers
like a damn Airbnb.

Jesus, look at that shade. But it could work.

Back to my bathroom, trying to blend the sickly
yellow-green of the bruise with the sparkly green of
the shadow, matching both eyes. It mostly hid the
bruising, but I looked like I'd fallen asleep on a dis-
eased avocado.

The sound of hammering from downstairs was,
for once, a welcome distraction. Ray, God bless him,
had arrived in some style at nine a.m. sharp, toolbox
in hand. I'd expected him to climb over the back
fence, but instead he'd walked all the way around the
block, past the media, and made a great show of set-

ting up his workstation on the sidewalk outside my house. When journalists started asking questions, he laid on the most ridiculous Speedy Gonzalez accent you ever heard, and pretended he barely spoke word one of English until the gentlemen of the press withdrew to their fishing chairs, and went back to cracking jokes about immigrants.

I wanted to help Ray out, but he whispered for me to keep out of sight, and the only assistance I could offer was leaving iced water just inside my door, while he finished his repairs. I was in the kitchen refilling when my phone buzzed on the counter.

Noah.

"Hey," he said, low and hushed against a background of faint, echoing coughs. I knew he was in some dusty corner of the library, yet something about his whispering made me think of drawn curtains and heavy sheets, of talking together in the dark. I didn't mind that idea.

"You at work?" I whispered back.

"I'm in the special collections archive. It's soundproofed. Mostly. I wanted to check in, see if you're okay after yesterday?"

I leaned against the counter, letting that warmth settle in. "Glad you did." Then I realized he meant the break-in, and hadn't even heard about my latest triumph with Paige. I guess he'd find out soon enough, because:

"Hey, Erin, do you want to do something later?" he asked.

"Yeah," I said, trying to sound casual. "Yeah, I'd like that. One thing though—fair warning—I'm experimenting with a new look."

I had to soften the blow of the eye somehow.

"Look forward to seeing it. I'll figure out somewhere to go, and message you. Gotta go, my boss looks like she's about to start alphabetizing my internal organs."

"Go," I laughed. "I'll see you later."

I hung up, a slow, unfamiliar smile spreading across my face. Every time we'd met since that night in The Canteen, it had been for a purpose. I needed a ride, he needed a book, we had to join forces to track down a maniac. The usual stuff. But this? This wasn't for any reason except fun.

Yet swirling underneath it all, the cold, heavy dread of the unanswered questions. Garrett. Eddie. The missing photo. The feeling that something was still out there, circling in the dark. Was this wise, going to a bar, wandering around downtown Lancaster?

I thought about texting Noah—somewhere between a casual, breezy message about drinks and a burger, and a police warning that our lives would be in constant danger. Finding the tone was a challenge, and I'd drafted and deleted it a dozen times, when a notification popped up on my screen. An email.

The sender was mgrieves@dominionoflight.org. The message was short, polite, and terminal.

Dear Miss Callahan,

Pastor DuMont was shocked and dismayed to see the recent footage of your altercation at the Cedar Ridge Elementary memorial. I'm sure you understand that Dominion of Light, as a pillar of this grieving community, cannot be associated with such behavior.

While we grieve alongside you, this public incident compels a time of reflection. Consequently, we have been forced to put your offer of employment on hold, until such time as we can seek

further spiritual and legal guidance on this matter.

Pastor DuMont and your mother
are, of course, still praying for
you. The offer to join our community will be reviewed, should
you choose to seek a more righ-
teous path. Until then, we are
keeping your file active.

Blessings,

Milton Grieves

Keeping your file active. I'd have taken it as a threat if
I didn't have bigger concerns right now. I could see
him, that bald little man in his sterile office, jacking
off to the power he had. His smug little face, the fingers of his free hand stroking that orange file—my
file, my family, my past, my future, ready to be used
against me whenever he saw fit.

But it didn't work. Instead, I got a liberating
sense of a bullet dodged. I didn't have to pretend
for Colleen anymore. The decision had been made
for me.

Of course, this meant I'd have the inevitable,

furious summons, demanding an explanation, accusing me of welshing on a deal with God, and now He wanted His five grand back. But the phone stayed silent. Maybe Grieves hadn't told her yet. Maybe even the Pastor of the Worship Dome was afraid to break this news to his most loyal soldier. That alone felt like a small, bitter victory.

But not much of one. Maybe I just didn't give a shit anymore. Maybe that was the solution to all of this—forget about being killed, ignore becoming a national pariah, just go out and have a drink. Not hammered, just a celebratory *you-can't-fire-me-I-quit* drink, and pretend to be wholesome and cut my food up small.

I just had to work around the eye, pick something to wear, and pretend none of it mattered.

By the time Noah's piece-of-junk car pulled up on Cherry Street, the edge-taking beer had turned into three, I was completely emotionally composed, and I was *not* just about to cry.

"You look nice," he said, as I clambered over the fence.

I stopped dead and glared at him. "I look like a fucking leprechaun." As I emerged out of the shadow of Ray's house, he saw right through my makeup and blinked.

"Okay," he said, rapidly adjusting to the new reality. "I see we've had another adventurous day."

"I told you I was trying out a new look."

He stepped closer, and winced at my eye.

"How did it happen?"

"Paige."

"The woman from the...?"

"Yep."

"Damn. Does it hurt?"

"Funnily enough, no. That's the thing about being punched in the face."

"Okay, stupid question."

"I've ruined our date."

He looked at me. "I just realized you're an idiot," he said, bluntly, and opened the car door. I turned on my heel and walked away.

"Where you going?"

"Maybe dial down the wit, Noah," I called. "I've heard getting kicked in the dick isn't much fun. Date's off."

He ran across Ray's lawn after me. "Erin, c'mon, I'm sorry. I just meant—we don't have to go anywhere you'll feel embarrassed."

I stared at him in disbelief. "I'll feel embarrassed *everywhere*. You think there's a bar in Ohio where I won't feel like a clown? Jesus Christ, Noah—you don't know women *at all*."

Undeterred, he rewound in his mind.

"What was that place you wanted to go to? That night when I picked you up outside the museum?"

I folded my arms.

"Alley Park Lake?"

"Yeah. The lake."

I drummed my fingers and made him wait.

"Okay. But if this is a date, you're buying beer. Stop at Kroger on the way."

We parked down by the Goslin Reserve. I drank two of our new beers, and then we took the quiet path, between the woods and the water, as the sun tilted down and the sky burned slowly orange. He remained a few feet from me, giving me space. I couldn't stop poking at my eye, and despite the green goblin mask, I felt oddly exposed in front of him.

I picked up a stick and tossed it into the lake. We

watched the ripples vanish.

"So what are you gonna do?" he asked. "About the job?"

I shrugged. "Mom gave me five grand to get back on my feet. Guess I'm gonna have to give it back to her. Whatever's left."

"How much did you spend?"

I didn't answer that, I just said, "I wonder if I could give her a kidney instead."

"Old people always need those."

We didn't speak for a moment. Then:

"Just keep the money, and we can use it to open a book club."

I snorted. "Books? In *this* place?"

And then I heard it.

We.

He'd said *we.*

"By the way, meant to tell you—'Vespiary'? Fucking good word."

Oh right—my dig at Demko. God, that seemed a year ago. What was it—two weeks?

"I saw it in a book," I said. "I have archives too."

"I like *clench.*"

"*Plinth.*"

"*Boondoggle.*"

"*Leg.*"

"*Leg?*"

"Try saying it ten times. It gets real weird real fast."

"Leg leg leg leg leg leg leg—oh man, that's nuts."

"Never argue with me, Noah Rafferty. I'm always right."

"Gotcha."

I turned out of the breeze and lit a cigarette.

"You're the only person I know who smokes."

"You're the only person I know with a moustache. Least ways, the only one who doesn't have a gun and a pickup."

"I don't know if I'm a gun and pickup kinda guy."

Not one bit.

I said, "I keep trying to quit. But you know—shit happens."

"Maybe try again when shit *isn't* happening?"

"Sure. I'll pencil that in for the day after never."

The wind shook the branches and startled up a flock of birds.

"Are there bears in these woods?" he asked.

"Dunno. Maybe. What would you do if there were?"

"Hit you with a shovel and save myself."

"Good answer." I was genuinely impressed. "Would you let me have a last cigarette between the shovel and Yogi getting me?"

He stopped. Looked into the trees.

"What?"

"...Nothing."

We kept walking.

I started twice, then decided to just go for it.

"There was a time when I quit. Years ago, for a few months—"

"So it *can* be done."

He'd never interrupted me before. I looked away, disappointed.

"Sorry," he said. "That was patronizing."

I nodded, still not looking.

"Sorry."

I nodded again—forget it. We were still brittle.

There's that *we* again.

He walked beside me in silence for a while.

"By the way," he said eventually, "*patronizing* is when someone explains things you already know."

Ah, you got me. *How can you not like this idiot?*

A twig cracked ahead of us, and a figure stepped out from the trees.

Red shirt.

Handgun.

I'd screamed at him in the street yesterday. Thrown cans. But now I knew him.

I knew him.

Eighteen, maybe twenty.

Miss Calley?

Noah grabbed the fabric of my skirt and pulled.

I'm scared.

The boy raised his arm.

"Hi, Mom."

And he fired.

Baby's Breath

Chapter 26: The Race

The sterile beep of a hospital monitor echoed down the corridor, rhythmic as a ticking clock. The bench I sat on was empty, except for me and the plastic cup of water a nurse had brought. Further down the corridor, through swinging doors, chaos—some car crash, some tragedy, somebody's life ruined in a moment.

Somebody else's.

In the other direction: emergency surgery.

I looked down at my hands. Blood turns grey-black under sodium lights. It was caked under my shaking fingernails. Blood and mud. I couldn't tell them apart.

I made my way to the restroom. Every light in this place was a punishment, and the ones above the sinks were no exception. The faucet spluttered, then ran cold over my wrists, and I watched, blank and wide-eyed, as pieces of Noah ran rosé-pink off my fingertips, thinning into the sink and away from me.

Nobody was listening, but just in case they

were——

"Please don't—please don't take him," I whispered. "Not this one too."

I'd known straight away that I wasn't hit, but I couldn't get up. By the time I was sure the shooter had gone, I was shaking too hard to stand. I'd had to crawl to Noah, scrabbling in the dirt. He was curled on the ground, both hands clutching his side——the right side, just below the ribs.

"What do I do? What do I do?"

He blinked up at me, trying to speak. I clamped my hands over his, as he banged his head on the mossy grass.

"Jeeesus, that hurts," he gasped.

He was turning white. Bleeding so much. It was pumping through his clenched fingers onto mine.

He was gonna die if we stayed here. Checked my phone—no signal up here. Would his be any different? I tried to turn him, to get into his back pocket where I'd seen him put it. Couldn't get him to roll. Probably wouldn't make a difference.

His car was——

Shit, where had we parked? I'd seen it, I'd known. Why couldn't I see it now?

Slow down. Get on top of this. Think.

Okay. Goslin Reserve. He'd parked near Goslin.

I set off running, but hadn't gone twenty paces before I realized there was no way I could get the car up here, and no way I could carry Noah all the way there.

Stop. Think.

Okay—I'd be better off running to Old Logan Road. Somebody would be driving by—I could flag them down, get help. I turned back, and as I ran past him, I realized I should tell him that this time, I wasn't just abandoning somebody to die.

"Noah—Noah!"

Was he unconscious, or just battling his pain?

I patted his face. Nothing. Slapped him hard. His eyes snapped open.

"What the fuck?"

"Shit, sorry! Noah, I have to go, I have to get help. I'll be back."

He just groaned.

"Don't you dare fucking die!"

Then I ran. Heart pounding. Brain screaming. Legs like knives. I'd promised those kids I'd hold things together, keep control, make it right for them and their parents. I'd failed every time. This time I could not fail. This time Noah depended on it.

Hi, Mom?

Oh God, don't die.

The trail became a track, then a path, then wide enough for tire ruts, and then I hit the tarmac. Empty. No cars.

Fuck fuck fuck fuck fuck.

Turned left. Right. Which way is my best bet?

I'd gone ten steps in the wrong direction when I heard an engine behind me.

Big red pickup. Perfect. I stepped into his path, hands raised, dead center, and strode towards him.

He'd stop for a bloodied woman, wouldn't he?

Or should I increase my chances, and get my tits out?

Didn't need to, he slowed anyway, a stunned look on his face. *Please be real, please be safe.* When he got out, I liked him immediately. A big, spare, middle-aged guy in a checked shirt. He'd do fine.

"You okay honey, are you hurt?"

"He's been shot." I pointed wildly. "He's been shot—my friend—he's back there."

He took the pickup as far along the path back to Noah as it could go, then we got out and ran—me fast, him trying to keep up.

Noah was out cold. He'd turned on his side, the wound to the sky.

Was that on purpose? Was that a good idea? Did that stop him bleeding?

God, but I loved how clever he is. He'd think of that. Wouldn't he?

"Where's the shooter?" he called, struggling up the path behind me.

"I don't—"

Oh god, is he gonna come back?

"It's okay, I don't see anyone. What's his name?"

"Noah."

"Noah." The guy crouched. "Noah, can you hear me?"

He checked the wound. Looked at me. Calm. Competent.

"It's okay, hon. I'm ex-military. I've seen worse, but I've seen better. We gotta get him up now. Gotta get him back to my truck."

We hauled Noah to his feet, just barely, with me handling him like china. Mostly the guy did it. I'd found some strength now, but it was raw, angry.

Hi, Mom?

Fuck! You!

We staggered up and down slopes, with tree roots and slippery grass fighting us every step.

"I'm Carl," he said.

Okay. Whatever, I don't give a good damn right now.

"You?"

"What?"

"Your name." He was panting. Ex-military or not, Noah was a dead weight.

"Erin."

The truck seemed twice as far as before, but we got there. Carl carefully put Noah's feet down, taking a breath while he figured it out. Front seat? Back seat? Bed of the pickup?

"Get the back door, Erin."

There it is again. Professional training. Repeat the name.

I'm scared.

Not now Della. Get out of my head. I can't manage both of you.

I opened the back door and Carl slid Noah's limp body inside. He checked for a pulse. Nodded, and reached for the driver's side.

"No."

He looked at me.

"Move. I'm driving. He's mine."

"It's my truck."

I don't know how I did it. My voice, I guess. My accusing, bloody finger in his face.

"I'm taking this fucking truck."

He blinked. Didn't move.

I stepped forward. Louder.

"I am taking. This fucking truck."

When Noah and I got to the hospital, I left the engine running, door swinging.

I didn't need to speak.

They saw my clothes.

A doctor in scrubs stepped into the room.

"Mr. and Mrs. Rafferty?"

They must've been here the whole time. I hadn't even heard them come in. He looked like Noah— the same slow, calm movements, the same clever eyes and hands, considering the world and handling it right.

She looked like hell had pitched a tent in her back yard.

I stepped closer.

"Okay," the doctor said gently. "You can breathe now. He's out of surgery. It was a difficult few hours, but he's stable and doing okay."

It felt like even the walls around us unclenched.

"The bullet entered just below the iliac crest— that's the top edge of the pelvis, right here". He pointed at his own hip. "It missed the abdominal cavity, and that's a big win. No major organ damage. However," he paused, and the room went cold again, "he's got considerable muscle trauma, and some bone trauma too. And there was a lot of contamination in the wound from the soil and fabric. We spent a long time cleaning it out to prevent infection."

"Is he going to be okay?" asked Noah's father.

"He was in hemorrhagic shock from blood loss when he arrived. We've transfused him, but that kind of thing—hard on the body. Right now, we've placed him in a medically induced coma. Sedated, on a ventilator. That'll be for maybe 72 hours. I know, it sounds scary, but it's a normal precautionary measure—it lets inflammation go down and gives him more time to stabilize."

"Can we see him?" she asked.

Can I see him too?

"Not yet. He's in the recovery room, and then in a little while we'll move him ICU. The nursing staff will get him situated down there, and they'll let you know as soon as you can go in. It's not gonna be today—but soon."

I dropped back into my chair, too heavy with relief to stand. The metal scraped the floor, and the doctor looked over.

"This is the woman who brought him in," he said.

They turned to me—the first time in weeks a stranger had looked at me without suspicion, or aiming a weapon.

He led his wife to me and laid a hand on my shoulder.

"Thank you," he said, his voice breaking. "Thank you for my son."

Baby's Breath

Chapter 27: The Benefaction

It didn't take long to talk ourselves out. We were spent. Silently drinking vending machine coffee when she strode in—determined, focused, loaded for war.

"Erin, I need to know what happened."

Demko was right behind her, but hardly looked at me. Straight to the nurse's station, notebook out, taking details, building a case.

Lomax didn't sit. Didn't soften her voice. She just stood there, broad and upright.

"He said—"

"Not here." She scanned the hall, grabbed my elbow, and led me to a small room, with blinds and a cross on the wall and two empty beds.

She looked at me. My eye.

"Were you hurt?"

"This? No, this was from... before."

"I told you not to go looking for him."

"I didn't! We were on a date."

"And your dad just—what—joined in?"

"It—wait, no, it's not him." The truth slipped out of me before I could brace for it.

Lomax's eyes narrowed. "Where's your father?"

I blinked, gathering myself.

"Your father, Erin, where is he?"

"I told you, it's not him!"

"He just shot Noah Rafferty, Erin! Don't waste my time!"

"He said he was my son."

"Bullshit. You don't have a son."

I closed my eyes.

Inhale. Hold. Exhale.

"Yes. I do. His name is Patrick. I named him after my grandfather."

There was a long silence. Even the air had paused.

"I was fifteen," I added. "They had him adopted. Dominion of Light. They found a couple. My mom's church. She handled it, found a place for him."

Lomax's voice was low. "No, we checked. When we got partial DNA match on your phone, we ran you, your parents. Nothing came back. No kids. No birth. No adoption record."

"They're sealed," I said. "I was fifteen and church girls don't get knocked up…" I looked away, remembering. "Mom told them—the cops—she said my dad had gotten me pregnant. That he'd… That he'd—"

I couldn't finish it. My throat shut tight.

"Don't do this," she warned. "Not now. We *know* your father was there—his DNA was all over your phone. In the classroom. At the scene."

I looked at her. *How can I make her believe me?*

I put my hand on her arm.

"I looked right at him—*today*. He was in the woods, and he—*for fuck's sake, listen to me!*" Her impatient eyes snapped back onto mine. "He shot Noah, right in front of me, at the lake. And he's not my dad, he's eighteen years old. He looks just like me, and he spoke to me—he said, 'Hi, Mom'."

The words landed in the small room and detonated. Lomax didn't speak. The suspicion didn't just drain from her face—it was ripped away. She took a single, involuntary step back, as if the air in front of me had caught fire. The authority, the certainty, the entire case she'd been building—it all collapsed in the space of a single heartbeat. For the first time, she looked at me not as a witness or a suspect, or even a victim. I was an epicenter.

"Gabi, listen," I said, pushing her to accept the truth, "I was fifteen and got pregnant, and Mom blamed my dad for... She kept me hidden for months until... this kid—this motherfucker... I'm telling you, he's my son, Gabi. That's why the DNA looks like mine."

"So... okay, so you're saying she told the cops it was your father? Your mom?"

I nodded.

"And the court sealed it? To protect you?"

"He never put a hand on me. I wanted to tell them, but my mom..."

I had to stop, but Gabi waited.

"She was part of the Church, you know. It's the goddamn Dominion of Light. Have you seen that place? They've got the Governor on speed dial, for Christ's sake. And... I was just a kid. She told the cops and the lawyers—and they bought it, 'cause it was the Church. They wouldn't even take my statement."

She stood there, eyes and ears finally open, mouth joining in. I'd told her this in Interview Room Four. She hadn't believed it then.

She believed it now.

"He's a good guy."

"He did eight years," she said, appalled.

"He didn't do anything wrong. They just—he had a copy of *Barely Legal* in his workbench, and that's all it took. She found it, and they bought it. Bought the story from Mom, from God, from a—" I could barely speak. "—from a fucking porn mag."

She nodded—short, shocked, jerky movements—looked at her notebook and back at me. I could see her thinking: *Who do I arrest for this?* But first—

"Who was the father?"

"It doesn't matter."

"Let *me* decide that."

"Please. He was just a kid. He left for college before any of this."

"I need his name, Erin. I have to act on this. I need evidence."

I knew who it was—but do I need to tell her? What good would it do now?

What good would it do to keep it a secret?

"He's called Danny Krawczyk."

As her pen moved, I reached across again and tried to pull away her wrist. She stepped back slightly.

"He never even knew I was pregnant."

Lomax's eyes were still on me. "Then who did?"

I stared past her. Past the brown walls and the crooked crucifix.

"Just me," I whispered. "Me. And the Church."

I swallowed. Then the truth finished itself.

"And Mom."

And it all came back—the months of shame, the years of guilt, the days of horror—collapsing at once.

The screaming fifteen-year-old—*let him stay.*

The terror in the school—*let them go.*

The fury at the lake—*let him live.*

All of it at once. It tore through me. Cracking me open, smashing my insides into shards, ripping me, shaking me loose. The dam was gone, but somehow I was still standing, staring right at who I wanted to kill the most.

She'd been waiting outside my life the whole time, patiently tapping her foot.

Of course she knew.

Of course she fucking knew.

She'd picked the parents. She'd made the calls. She'd told the story that sent Dad to prison. She *liked* the neatness of it, the purity. She found sin growing inside my changing body, and put it away from us both, and then because she was on a roll, she found another sin in dad. So he had to go too.

She cleaned her life up with mine, left me with a gap the size of a begging bowl, desperate to be filled.

She's spotless because I'm filthy.

The thought wasn't mine. It belonged to my very bones, and now it was screaming. The need to move, to act, to outrun the shaking in my own hands was overwhelming.

I shoved the chair back so hard it crashed against the wall, the noise ripping through the quiet room.

"Erin," Lomax said, startled.

"I have to go."

"Where are you going?"

I didn't answer.

"Erin, I can't let you leave."

But I was already out the door, down the stairs, with Lomax's voice echoing behind me, chasing me out into the parking lot.

The stolen pickup was still where I'd abandoned

it. I still had the keys, cold in my hand. The steering wheel, sticky with drying blood.

I turned it anyway.

Hi, Mom?

Fuck you. Fuck you. You're no part of me. Not now.

Colleen could wait. She'd get hers next.

But first I was going back to find him. Back to the scene of the shooting.

Chapter 28: The School

I'd driven in, even though I usually walked on days like this. My shoulder still ached from carrying home twenty-seven books in a tote with frayed straps, marked homework and half-finished drawings poking out the top. A plastic folder of lesson plans had fallen flat in the back seat. I told myself I'd bring it in during recess. There wouldn't be a recess.

I parked under one of the maples that edged the staff lot, already dreading the weight of everything I'd have to carry home. I was too tired the night before, when Eddie had called. Tonight I'd be even worse. But it was Friday soon.

The sun was out early, spilling warm across the sidewalk, dappling the red bricks. Birds were louder than usual, or maybe it was a day that called more attention to them. I should get the kids out on the grass later, get them drawing blue jays.

Inside, the halls still smelled like dry erase markers and someone's too-early popcorn. Fran Loxton was already at the mail cubbies.

"You look like you slept in your car," she said, grinning.

"Didn't. Would have, given the chance."

"Don't forget—cake in the staff room at 3:45. Janelle's birthday."

"Right. Cake. I'll be there."

We headed to class together, swapping shorthand about our evenings. Her husband had fallen asleep in front of *Dateline* again. I told her I'd eaten cereal for dinner and graded twelve spelling tests before passing out. She took over the register while I unpacked the books.

The classroom was still, soft with morning light. Our calendar was set to May, but the theme board still had faded cut-outs from April showers. I flipped the switch on the AC unit—still dripping. I'd have to speak to Darnell. Again.

Morning meeting. The kids filed in, backpacks thumping, sneakers squeaking. Mason tried to show me something on his phone before I confiscated it. Kara had forgotten her glasses again. Rafael had a Band-Aid across one cheek, and apparently no idea how it got there.

We started with the Pledge. Caleb forgot to put his hand over his heart, then caught himself halfway through. Della, in her knitted octopus sweater, eight legs hugging her tight, was whispering to Maisie, who was whispering to God knows who. I made a mental note to split them up for reading.

I stood in my usual place, and spoke my usual bouncy line.

"One two three, and eyes on me."

A quiet hush settled. Almost reverent.

I moved among them, checking the night-before reading logs. Half weren't signed. Grace had a note from her mom saying they'd had a family emergency. I squeezed her shoulder.

"Good job just being here."

Math came next. I handed out the worksheets while Fran took the lunch count. Tom and Evan needed help with basic subtraction, so I crouched beside them, walking them through it. Devon was already halfway done, smudging graphite over his page with the side of his hand. Lashka tapped her pencil like a woodpecker.

"Less noise, more thinking," I said, and smiled.

By mid-morning they were buzzing. Della floated from desk to desk, showing off her new pockets with unfeigned, unselfish delight. Her mom had sewn them into her bottle green skirt, and they stuck out, bright, vulgar orange tongues that she simply couldn't stop playing with.

"They go all the way down," she beamed. "Look! You can hide a rock in here! Or snacks! Or two whole fingers!"

"Don't hide fingers, Del," I said. "You'll need those for coloring later."

She nodded solemnly and went off to inform someone else.

Lunch. Some had PB&Js, burritos wrapped in foil, Ziplocks of carrot sticks. Maisie had her usual plastic tray, untouched. Salad. She scowled at it like it had personally insulted her.

"I'm not hungry," she said.

"Me neither," I said, and sat down beside her with a granola bar.

I took a bite. She took a bite. One for one. Our routine.

Tom was caught taking a chocolate bar out of Devon's bag. Both boys cried. I separated them, gave them space, brought them back together once they'd cooled. Tom said sorry. Devon said sorry too, then realized that for once, he didn't need to, and sulked. They didn't hug, but they sat beside each other at the table like nothing had happened.

The class always got drowsy after lunch, so we

never tried to do much with them. Today was no different. Heads lolled. Chairs squeaked. I dimmed the lights just a little, handed out pencils and printed mandala sheets to color. Something simple, while I pinned another half dozen drawings to the walls, and opened windows to the cooling breeze.

Fran popped her head in on her way to a meeting. "Still cake later?"

I gave her a thumbs-up and went back to handing out the last of the pencils. I liked this peaceful, sleepy hour after lunch. I got a moment to myself, just a short second to look outside. Sun poured over the lawn. The grass was patchy, but green. A white-haired woman walked her equally elderly dog slowly along Mill Hollow. A guy in a red hoodie headed the other way, along the edge of the playground, hands deep in his pockets, and then Grace began to cry, and I turned to see what the latest disaster was.

The AC had dripped. Again. A dot of water had smeared Grace's careful purple sunburst, ruined, and she wailed at the betrayal.

"Never mind, sausage," I said, reaching for tissues. I hugged her one-armed, automatic.

Fran was back by now, so I asked if she'd mind talking to Darnell about the air conditioning this time. "He never does a thing for me, but I think he's scared of you."

"So he should be," she said, told the children she'd be right back, and stepped out the door. I glanced at the clock. 1:41. Almost reading time.

I'd just got them settled with their books, when somewhere down the corridor a voice was raised, echoing down to Lightning Bugs. Devon and Tom were easily distracted and looked up, pleased that they'd have something to focus on that wasn't work.

I heard a man's voice—*fuck you*. And what sounded like a shocked cry.

A bang, something slamming, perhaps. Voices raised, and that bang repeated. The empty halls always echoed, so I couldn't place the sound, but I turned away from the kids, listening for the source.

Next door, maybe. Through the wall I heard the door crash open, and a chair scrape across the floor. Then Steve Dublin's voice—*stop stop stop*, and now, unmistakable, a gunshot.

And then the screaming started.

This morning they'd all been breathing, breathing, breathing so much that I'd opened the windows wide enough to accommodate it all. A breeze had swept in, lifting their drawings off the walls, crepe-paper art waving a desperate warning at them that a murderer was about to come into the room.

Why didn't I listen?

I froze. Four huge shots, each an enormous noise, and then an eerie silence that wasn't a silence at all. Pounding in my ears, and the muffled sound of hollering and crying. Somebody pulled at me, and I looked down. Della's hand, a tiny fist wrapped around my skirt. She was mouthing my name.

What?

"Miss Calley."

I looked up, and everything slid into place again.

"Not now."

Some of the kids had vanished under desks as we'd practiced. Others stared at me, unsure.

"Hide," I said. Shouted. It was too loud. Some began to cry.

"I'm scared."

Della was still there. Her eyes were huge.

Run. That single word screamed at me. That animal instinct. Get out. Save yourself.

Stay. That small hand, twisted. Stay with the kids. Protect.

Run. Stay. Help. Run. My fingers, a blur, found my phone.

Nine.

One.

One.

The door opened and he stepped inside, with his sleeves rolled up, ready for work.

I flung the phone at him. Hit him.

Fucker didn't even look at me.

The gun went off—straight into the rows of tiny desks, blowing the breath right out of the room. Between two racing heartbeats I dropped to the ground. Steve's room had been loud enough. When it was our turn the sound itself was a violence, a shocking slap of noise so huge it felt like something living. It seemed realer than the figure who stood above me, legs wide and all mechanics, his shots precisely timed and spaced, metronomic.

Into the desks. Into the walls. Into the kids. Wood splintered. Breath punched out of lungs. Screams. Wet sounds. A spatter of red across drawings and clothes.

Della was screaming. "Miss Calley, Miss Calley, Miss Ca—"

A splash of heat on my face.

And then, when he'd done what he came here to do, he stepped over me and walked out.

I scrabbled in the blood. And I left them. I ran.

Down the hallway, over Steve, his body like dropped laundry. I slid across linoleum and crashed through doors, heading out of the dark and into the light by the school lobby, where Janelle was pulling herself, red, into a corner.

Double doors and blinding daylight. I heard a voice screaming and knew it was me. I turned left, across the field, the field where I'd seen the man walking—no, wait, he'd see me if I came this way. Turning as I fell, I skidded on the slippery grass and hauled myself up again. There was a siren in the distance, and I headed that way, towards the school gates. A woman with a dog reached out to me, but I dodged her and kept racing onto Mill Hollow.

Legs pumping acid, lungs on fire, I ran shrieking toward the police cruiser as it skidded to a halt. Two cops were heading my way, the youngest, his gun already drawn, all fear and courage, racing towards hell. He caught me, didn't say a word, just bent me double and we sprinted together up Mill Hollow, towards the gathering forest of flashing blue lights.

"I left them," I gasped, and dropped to the sidewalk.

The sun was still shining. Like nothing at all had happened.

Like it was still the kind of day you'd get the kids

out to draw birds.

Chapter 29: The Clearing

The woods didn't answer. They never do.

But the trees—God, the trees—they *listened*. Withholding, ancient, patient. The trail curved inward like a hook, taking the last of the light with it. Dragging it away into the darkness to consume.

I stood alone in the hush, fists balled, shoulders trembling, breath clouding in the cooling, stilling air. Even bellowing, my voice felt too small for what I needed it to carry, but I let it out anyway.

"Get your ass out here!"

Nothing. Just leaves whispering and the earth pretending it hadn't seen. I walked twenty more paces. Every step like testing the surface of a frozen lake.

"Come on, then! I'm *waiting!*"

The last word tore at the edge of my voice. Still nothing. The silence twisted in me like a blade, cruel and slow, making me feel every cold, sharp second.

"I SAID—" My voice cracked. *"MOMMY'S*

HERE!"

That did it.

A sound. A rustle. And then—

He appeared.

Thirty, forty feet ahead, he grew out of the gloom like it was giving birth to him—slow, rotting, inevitable. Like this was always gonna happen. Like that's just how nature works. He didn't step. He *unfolded* from the dark, like the forest had been holding him in reserve. Red hoodie. Pale skin. The easy, boneless sway of someone without fear. One hand empty. One hand not.

"Hi, Mom," he said, soft as milk.

I couldn't breathe. Backbones are the original bones, the first to evolve, the first to grow. A billion years of perfection, and yet mine barely held me now. Only willpower kept me upright. The air felt thick, unnatural, like I was underwater. Like I'd screamed open a dam and it had dragged me under.

But I steadied myself. I knew this feeling—the hollow ache of him. It was born the same day he was, in a room that smelled of antiseptic and incense. That void I'd carried all these eighteen slow years— that begging-bowl hole—it stood in front of me now, here on this heath, under the rising, gazing moon. Made flesh, yet just as vacant as it had ever been.

"Hello, Patrick."

His tone was flat, instructive—a patient teacher helping a slow child to catch up. "No," he frowned, "my name's Elias."

He took a step forward, closing the distance between us, like a correction.

"You were Patrick to me," I said. "That's what I called you, in the womb."

He nodded his encouragement, and walked further towards me, slowly conspiring, sharing a dark joke. "It's okay, I get it. We all make mistakes. Call me Patrick, if it helps."

"What are you doing here, Elias?"

"Call me Patrick, though. Patrick is better. It's like... our thing." He smiled—not like Eddie or Ty, or Noah. Not like anybody else but me. His smile was made of mirrors.

But this—this wasn't anything I'd made.

"Elias—"

"No!" he said, not loudly, just sharply. "You call me Patrick. That's what I want."

I hadn't blinked. Not since he emerged. I kept all my focus on him as he moved forward, like a sinuous, clammy, fungal thing, reaching out to me.

But then he softened again. "Glen and Beth, they don't like me talking about you. But we can have this together. Patrick. Like a secret."

"And Glen and Beth are…"

"They're my mom and dad. But they don't like me to call them that. My other mom and dad, not my real ones."

"Okay… Patrick…" I said, carefully repeating my question: "What are you doing here?"

His tone shifted. Grew. Up on high now, like he'd seen somebody play this part, spotted it in an old movie of a teacher in a gown, chastising a pupil.

"The thing is, things were getting out of control. I think we both know that much."

My throat tightened.

"You mean… with Glen and Beth?"

"No," he interrupted, irritated at my stupidity. "With you! Your life. It was a mess."

"My life…?"

"I've heard," he said. "You'd be amazed what I know. That you were letting yourself go. Going off the rails. She said. And someone had to step in. Someone had to make things right."

My heart hammered. *She…?* Couldn't be…

I tried to say something, to ask the question, but my throat was a knot of ice and fury. He watched me—then tilted his head, a new thought breaking across his face.

"Sorry about your boyfriend," he said, suddenly, shattering my thought, pushing me off balance. He sounded almost bashful. "I didn't want to hurt him. He was just in the way."

"You were aiming for *me?*"

Oh God, this is how I die.

But he frowned, looking around at the trees—searching for some sane soul to back him up. "No. I mean, he was in the way of *us*. Us being together again. Like Granny said."

And now the name hit me sideways. Granny?

"What did you just say?"

No—

No—No no no—

"What did you just say?"

"She told me," he continued, his eyes gleaming with gospel and rot. "She wrote and said you were getting off the right path. You were drifting, and... A woman needs guidance from a man." Here endeth the lesson. "And you didn't have a proper man around, just wastrels. I liked that word. Anyway, she said I should come back into your life."

Colleen, in my ear: *I'm trying to bring Him back into your life.*

I thought she'd meant God. She'd conjured the Devil.

I bent double, shaking. It rose up inside me, but I clamped it down—jaw locked, fists tight.

"Mom?" he said, taking yet another step closer, looking genuinely concerned. "Are you okay?"

"I'm not—" panting now, my voice scraping low, "I'm not your fucking mother."

How the hell do you deal with a crazy person in the woods? The way he did it was this—calm as a prayer: "You are. For real. Glen and Beth, they don't get me, I knew you would."

The ground under my feet swayed.

"You killed them."

He looked puzzled.

"No. They're back in Michigan."

Screaming at him now.

"No not—*fuck's sake*, I don't give a shit about Glen and Beth, you crazy bastard! She stole you from me! I meant *my* kids," and I hammered my hand on my chest. "You killed *my* kids, my class."

"Them?" *How could I still be worried about them?* "I cleared the way. For us. For you."

"Cleared? You murdered seventeen people, you crazy fuck!"

His whole posture changed. The child was gone. Another step forward, hard and sudden, toe-to-toe. His gun hand was still hanging by his side, but his free hand jabbed the air in front of my face, like a courtroom accusation.

"You don't talk to me like that!" he snarled. "I am your SON!"

"But I am NOT your mother!" I bellowed.

"YES. YOU. ARE." He raised his arms, waiting for the praise, shouting it for himself in the meantime. "I risked everything for us. That's what real men do! They take care of what's theirs, and they make things right!"

"What's *yours*? I'm not *yours*."

He was on his toes in front of me. "A WOMAN NEEDS A MAN!"

He turned away in disgust, stomping up the hill as if the argument was won. But he was wrong. He wasn't a man. He was a boy playing with a gun, spouting words his grandmother spoon-fed like poison. He was an excuse. A twisted absolution for her own sins. And I would not let him be mine.

I marched right after him and—gun or not—when he heard me he stepped back. I stopped, barely three feet in front.

"You think *this* makes you a man?"

We stood, breathing hard, the clearing pulsing with unspoken violence. The trees waiting, uneasy. This place was a courtroom, a church, and a graveyard all at once.

"They were in the way, mom" he finally mumbled, petulant.

"In the—*don't call me that*," I snapped. His head jerked back as if slapped. He glared at me. "In the way of what?"

"I told you. Of *us*."

I put my head in my hands, and we stood under the moon, silently.

"And what about Ty Holcomb?" I finally asked. "What had he done?"

"Which one was that?"

"*Which one was that?*"

"Oh, him. Well, he treated you like a whore," he said, like that settled the matter. "I watched how he treated you that day."

"That day?"

"After I did the school."

That day. The day I borrowed Arnie's car. The day I visited Mom. The day I saw the orange file on her personal shrine to the Dominion of Light.

It all tumbled into place.

The flowers. The card. The file on Milton Grieves' desk—that bright orange twin of the one in Colleen's parlor. That's who *She* was, to Patrick. My mother. She'd summoned *this* to my school. She'd found a monster, convinced herself he'd heal her guilt, and called him back from the dead.

"You sent the flowers. The baby's breath."

"Did you like them?"

I turned away, maybe to vomit. He could shoot me right now, with my back to him, and I'd never know. And right at that moment, I didn't care. If I died, fine. I'd made this, or half of it at least. I deserved whatever came. But I didn't want to die without answers. I walked down the hill, forming my thoughts, waiting for the shot I might not even hear. On the ground ahead of me, a black stain. We were at the spot where Noah had stood, had fallen, might never stand again.

"And you shot him."

"Yeah, but you know he's married?"

"No—you shot *him*," I said in a low growl, pointing at the bloody grass. "Oh, you fucker, you shot my Noah."

"Sure. But you can love me now."

Somewhere behind me, a breeze shifted. The forest flinched.

"You think this is love?"

In the distance, a sound—sirens.

"What aren't you getting? I thought you'd say thank you."

"You're out of your goddamn mind."

"But I killed them for *you*," he said, whining like I'd cheated at some agreed transaction.

The sirens were closer now, curling through the trees. She'd followed me. *Thank God,* Lomax had followed me from the hospital. He finally heard them, his eye shifting, a flicker of confusion crossing his face. The real world was finally breaking through.

"They're coming for you, Patrick," I said quietly, pointing over my shoulder at the trap about to close, just as Gabi had in Interview Room Four, pinning my every flaw on me like a badge. "So let me say it for the record."

I closed in on him, and my finger stabbed the air like a blade.

"I don't love you."

Closer.

"I want you dead."

Closer.

"And I hope, this time, that *they kill you for me.*"

He didn't shout. Didn't argue. His mouth turned into a sulk, he stepped back into the trees, and he was gone.

Baby's Breath

Chapter 30: The Inheritance

The manhunt was underway. They had him now: a name, a description, a witness, a reason. They even had the DNA—pound upon pound of it, scraped from me, and by extension, from Colleen.

The only thing they didn't have was him. Ten feet into the woods, the leaves swallowed every footprint. By the time I came screaming down the path—a wild-eyed banshee flinging myself into the headlights, gasping and pointing into closing darkness—Patrick was gone.

Demko was out of his car first—low, fast, gun drawn. He didn't stop for me. It wasn't until he was sure the area was safe that he led us back up the hill, Lomax and me, her arm around me, him asking me to show where the shooter had gone into the trees.

I don't think Demko knew how to touch humans, or maybe he's not allowed. But Lomax—she held me.

Held me as I howled—over what I'd just said to my own child.

Held me through eighteen years.

Held me while I broke.

She didn't take a statement, not then. She just held me and listened, waiting for the waters to subside.

The troops gathered. First, a black-and-white, then more, which Demko organized into a search of the woods, and the return of poor Carl's pickup. Then overhead, a helicopter tearing in from Columbus—spotlights blazing, drowning out my sobs. And finally, Gabi led me down the path, back to Goslin Reserve, to the ambulance that was waiting for me. Back to the soft sanctuary of sedation. And overhead, in the woods, along every path and every hiding spot, the search continued.

The two days after the manhunt began were a void. The news vans were a permanent fixture on the horizon, but their hunger felt distant. I slept in ragged snatches, waking to the phantom sound of sirens. I held the book Noah once left on my kitchen counter—held it without opening it, and then set it aside. Read the same page of a magazine a dozen times. Ray brought over more food I couldn't eat. The silence in the house was a physical weight. So when Gabi called, the sound of the phone was a shock, a sudden intrusion from a world that had felt like it was moving on without me.

It was the first of many calls, updating me. In the

time it took for the full weight of law enforcement to arrive, he'd turned back into air. Patrick—Elias—whoever was living in that head I'd bequeathed him, was a ghost again. They found tire imprints in the mud—maybe his, maybe not. Could've belonged to any one of ten models, and as the tracks bled into the tarmac of the road, they faded to nothing in a hundred feet.

Sometime that first evening they found a temporary camp, not even in a clearing—just a tree with a kid's two-man tent under it, and some junk food and candy wrappers. Lying in the dirt, near the hole he'd dug for his toilet, the framed photo of my dad and I hugging on a shoreline when I was just fourteen, and stolen from the yellow dresser. They tagged it as evidence—the only piece of Garrett I had left. The only piece, until someone actually bothered to track the old man down.

And whose priority was that, now?

The media frenzy got up pace, and transformed into something at once pin-sharp in my senses, and entirely abstract. The hero who became a bitch was now something conceptually new, something too bizarre to slide into the usual classifications. No single news ticker could explain it. Ray told me Channel 9 ran a two-hour special.

They didn't get any new footage of me, though.

Gabi had gotten me home before the news vans had their satellites aimed, for which I thanked her in my own mind, whenever I remembered, and cursed her for the rest of the time. I was trapped again, a creature in a cage, this time with a police guard posted at the end of my walkway.

But at least I wasn't a suspect anymore. Never was, Demko told me at some point in this nevertime. They hadn't ever thought I was, not really, not even during that interrogation in Interview Room Four. That's what cops do. Squeeze and see what leaks out.

What a consolation prize.

Now, though? The news couldn't classify me, and nor could the police. Part of my new identity was *victim*. Another part: *mother of a missing person*. Every day brought a fresh, pointless update, either from the cops, or—as they moved onto new traumas destroying different lives—from the TV news.

None of it added up to anything. The neat endings they sell you in movies are a lie. In real life, horror just limps forward until it blends into normal. I sat and drank coffee and tried not to smoke too much, channel-hopping, then switching away again quickly every time I saw my face.

Two days after they called off the search of the woods, a different familiar face took me by surprise.

I sat up suddenly and turned on the sound.

He wore a somber suit and tie, with plain white ribbon draped around his neck as he delivered the last rites to my mother, in a prepared statement for the media.

"Like all people of faith," said Pastor DuMont, "We have watched the aftermath of the Cedar Ridge tragedy with broken hearts. Our prayers—and our resources—have gone out daily to those grieving. Yet the media have repeated scurrilous rumors that a woman—" he paused to check he was getting this complete stranger's name right "—a Ms. Colleen O'Brien, implicated in this atrocity, had at one time attended services at our church. I have no recollection of ever having met Colleen O'Brien. While we trust in God's mercy, we also believe in accountability. Ms. O'Brien is no longer welcome in our church, and we disavow her actions. Dominion of Light will continue to work with law enforcement agencies to ensure she is held to account—"

I turned the TV off.

DuMont's methods were brutal enough for me to wonder if Colleen had orchestrated them herself.

Not even Cherry was a safe route out of my home that first week. The cameras had figured it out—my low-fence shortcut—and set up with long lenses, fifty yards from the Garcia plot. That was as close as Lomax let them get. Ubers were out, unless they came with tinted glass. So I called Ray—for the thousandth favor.

He didn't seem to mind. Told me he liked the kid.

I lay flat in Ray's back seat until we were past the cameras.

Last time I came this way, I was in the back of an ambulance, soaked in Della's blood. Time then had split wide open like a rotten seam. Now, it ticked forward again—but the best part of me was still in pieces.

I needed to see him.

Ray waited in the lot while I pulled up my hood and slipped inside. The ICU was on the third floor, behind a locked door, and I had to wait while a nurse buzzed me through.

I gave his name. She checked a list, then pointed me to his room.

Through the wired glass panel, I could see him— blanketed badly, his arms flat at his sides, his mouth open, a slight frown. The ventilator was gone, they told me, but he was still sedated. The tube had bruised his throat; even if he woke up, he wouldn't be able to speak for days.

That suited me fine. I was saving my words. I just needed to be near him.

He had an oxygen pipe under his nose, rattling a snore so I'd know he was still in there. I stroked his wrist lightly. Nothing. So I let him rest.

Even though he couldn't hear me, I told him I was still trying to get through *We Are Animals*—that dumb book about the fucked-up family. I doubted I could finish it even on my best days. And these were not my best days. Fortunately the waiting room had the latest *Marie Claire*, so I read that instead.

When the nurse came in, I looked up and smiled.

"Hi," I said.

She smiled back, efficiently, checked the monitors, scribbled something on his chart, then turned to me.

"I don't think we've met?"

"No. It's my first visit."

"You're...?"

"Erin."

"Erin Callahan?"

"Yes."

"I saw you on the news."

No escape.

"Are you family?"

"No. I'm—" I hesitated. "I was the one who brought him in."

She paused, softened. "Sorry, hon…"

I nodded. Stood up. Squeezed his hand goodbye.

I took the *Marie Claire* home with me.

Fuck 'em.

I didn't hear from Gabi Lomax for a few days. Instead, Demko called with minor updates. Once, he showed up. Didn't sit—just stood in the hallway, facing into my room, so I couldn't sit on my sofa and still make eye contact with him. I stood instead, braced.

"Elias—Patrick—"

We still hadn't agreed what to call him.

"—he had a phone."

"Okay."

"The FBI have been tracing his activity. Sorry it's taken a while. It's no longer such an urgent case, now he's…"

Dead? Disappeared? Already someone else?

"His internet history—it's interesting. He's spent a lot of time on YouTube, TikTok, socials. Erin… ever heard of the manosphere?"

It was like being questioned.

Yes, I've heard of the manosphere.

Do I need a lawyer?

"He'd spent a lot of time on websites and channels associated with that stuff. Cage fighters and… they're scammers, mainly. Drumming up donations or clickbaiting. Anyway—"

"So that's it? A school shooter was an incel? Is that the big news?"

He took off his glasses and looked down, cleaning them rigorously with a neatly folded handkerchief from his pocket.

"You know," he said, head still down, "none of this is your fault."

He looked up at me.

"I just thought you should know."

A week later, Demko called again. Somebody walking a dog had found a gun in an old, abandoned Honda parked by Buckeye Lake. Patrick's fingerprints were everywhere. The driver's door was still open.

The lake is vast. And who knows: maybe he was never in there at all.

Anyway, they pulled the divers out after two days.

This got the news interested one last time. They hammered on my door the moment the beat cop outside went for a toilet break. I told all of them no—not even at the new, even higher price. After that, they stopped asking, and almost overnight, they vanished. If anyone hated me now, at least I knew it was personal—not just for ratings.

And that was that.

My son was taken from me.

Then he came back—

And now he was gone again.

A couple of days later, Gabi called and asked me to meet her at Holm Coffee on King Street for lunch. I hesitated, but she said she was buying, so I walked there, through clean air sweeping down from the Appalachians.

"A crazy person can come from anywhere," she told me over open sandwiches and latte. "You did nothing wrong."

"I've been hearing that ever since I ran away from Della Morrison," I said.

"It's still true."

I looked over her shoulder at the high street outside, ordinary life going on.

"So if nobody did anything wrong, how come…?"

All this.

"Sometimes shit just happens."

"I guess. But my mom's genes probably didn't help."

"Your mom's not crazy."

"She faked being a Baptist for eighteen years."

"She did that, yeah."

"*What the actual fuck.*"

She just sat and chewed on it. I liked her steady pace through life. All about finding the right answer.

"It takes a while to get to sealed records," she said.

"It takes time and rank. Honestly, I wish my guys were half as determined."

"Eighteen years of pretending, though?"

"I've known people do it longer."

I looked at her.

"This place…"

She trailed off, searching for the words.

"You get tired of trying to fit. You learn to hide things. Doesn't always come from a bad place."

I held her ringless hand across the table.

She let go first.

"So what happens to her?"

"Your mom? Dunno. We're looking at charges for aiding and abetting, but—"

"But?"

"She contacted him—we can prove that. Dozens of emails. But there's nothing to show she helped him once he got to Ohio. Hard to prove she knew what he was going to do, either before or after. Might collapse before trial."

She paused.

"We could've charged her for concealing the pregnancy, but statute of limitations ran out. Prosecutors are considering fraud, but I doubt we'd get a conviction for pretending to be more religious than she really is. Around here? Who isn't?"

"So she just gets away with it?"

She gave a small shrug.

"I dunno. What laws did she really break?"

I let out a dry laugh. "God's?"

She finished her coffee and stood.

"We all do that, honey."

I heard his adoptive parents, Beth and Glen, had signed a deal—tragedy and grief in a neat little package, with ad breaks. But I had no feelings left to feel about any of it.

People are going to be good, or they're going to be greedy assholes. Nothing I can do.

All I knew was this: the woods lay bare, his car vacant, his gun abandoned, his digital life swept clean. Patrick was gone, if he had ever existed.

But at least they found my father.

Gabi called with the news, and this time, when I walked out of my front door to my own car, the street was quiet. I drove to my mother's neighborhood, the perfect gardens and silent houses feeling more like a cemetery than ever.

Her lawn was three inches too long, browning near the edges. She didn't answer the front door, so I unlatched the side gate and went around to the back. There she was, sat in her parlor on one of those stupid, ugly, Louis the Whatever-the-fuck chairs, looking out onto the garden.

She saw me, lifted her chin, held my gaze, blinked first, and came to let me into the kitchen.

"Heard they bailed you."

"It's absolutely ridiculous," she sniffed, walking away, her voice brittle. "I had nothing to do with any of this."

I didn't reply. She reached the stove and stood, holding the edge of it, her back to me. Silence. Two strangers in a kitchen, with an abyss between us.

"So you're not even going to offer me a coffee?"

I finally said.

"I'm out of everything," she replied without turning around. "I don't have coffee. I don't even have bread."

"I'm not here to do your shopping for you, Colleen."

"I never liked you calling me that. What's wrong with 'Mom'?"

Everything. Every dead inch between us. Every footstep behind. That's what's wrong with Mom.

"Forget the coffee. Let's sit down anyway," I said, pushing past her into the parlor and settling onto the sofa. She followed, a stiff procession of one, and took her usual chair.

"I got some news," I told her. "They found dad."

She snorted. "That man."

I let the silence stretch until it was uncomfortable. Until she had to make the effort, to look away from the window and settle on me.

"He's dead."

She stared, her face a blank canvas. No shock. No grief. Nothing.

I took a moment, remembered the lines I'd practiced on the way over.

"They found him in a car outside Sugar Grove. He'd been working on a construction job down there. A utilities worker found him. Looked like he'd parked off a service road to sleep without being moved on."

I thought for a moment about telling her more. Telling her that Noah and I had tried to find him, but this job wasn't on our list. The site had been mothballed two months earlier. It wasn't part of Noah's archive.

But I decided she didn't deserve any part of Noah.

"The cops tracked down the site manager. He said Dad just didn't come into work one day. They figured he'd moved on. Happens a lot."

I looked for any sign on her face, any crack in the fortification she had built. Nothing.

"I spoke to Gabi Lomax—you know Detective Lomax, of course…"

She made a tiny sniff.

Yeah. You do. I let myself have a small, cold smile.

"She said they couldn't be sure how long he'd been

there. It was hard to tell because… well, it's just hard to tell. The heat, and the back of a car. But weeks, she said. He wouldn't have been alive to hear about any of this. But they found angina meds with him. Looks like natural causes."

The only natural thing about this family.

Birdsong drifted through the window. My mother looked older, frailer than I'd ever seen her. Her usually perfect hair was uneven, clearly a home job, and the brave, powdered mask she'd painted on to face the solitude was beginning to crack.

"He didn't deserve that," she said, in a whisper as dry as Bible paper. I looked up, hoping I'd finally see a conscience.

But no. "Not after what he did," she said.

What he did? There she sat, the woman who had sacrificed my innocent father to save her own reputation, given away my child to maintain her social status, summoned a monster to soothe her guilt, who had broken every life she'd ever touched.

And I felt… nothing.

The anger was gone, burned out, leaving only a cold, vast emptiness.

"Goodbye, Colleen," I said, and walked out.

It was the last time I ever saw her.

So she never got to find out the rest of it. That Dad had died in squalor, in a broken-down car with bald tires and a new battery and a failing heart, trying to get back to me. She had no right to his final moments, no right to any more of his story, no right to his life. Nor to his afterlife.

And she certainly had no right to know about his money. Died alone, in a sleeping bag in the back of a car, yet he'd been sitting on nearly eight thousand dollars. He'd left it all to me.

That's how my father showed he still loved me.

So to show I loved him back, I spent some of his eight grand having his remains brought to Lancaster for cremation. After two decades cast out at the hands of Colleen's civilized, corporate Christianity, he deserved to come home.

I was still keeping out of sight, my eye still bruised, my feelings still raw. So I'd organized everything online or over the phone, finding the cheapest place in town, and both me and Ray—who volunteered to drive me—were confused by the location my phone map sent us to. We drove around the block three times until we realized—yep, this really is it. Just an office, tucked in a strip mall, with a dusty sign above the door.

Ray asked if I'd like him to come in with me, for company, to show respect.

"Thanks, Ray, but you didn't know him."

"Sure, but I know you."

I paused, hugged him, and went inside alone.

The place was called Legacy Funeral Services, although God knows what the legacy was. A murderous grandson, a prison record, and a fuck-up in a sixty-dollar funeral suit. Inside, the place smelled like the nail salon next door. A bored woman at the desk explained, with an indifference that takes years to perfect, that they didn't actually do cremations on site. This was just the office.

"We have a facility out of town," she said. "But we can bring the remains here for you on..." she checked a calendar on her screen, "the nineteenth." She looked up at me and removed her glasses. "Or we can have them mailed."

While I thought about it, I could sit in a room

labeled *A Moment of Grace*, the name stuck in a plastic frame. Through the door was a small and beige room with eight chairs in two rows, plastic ferns and generic art on the walls. I was supposed to feel something in here—grief, anger, relief—but all I felt was the quiet hum of the air conditioner. I briefly looked through the book of poems, each page laminated like a shopping catalog, until I came across one branded with the all-too-familiar dove and cross.

I shut it. Paid the bill. Left.

The late afternoon sun was still high, but declining into the muggy heat of Lancaster. I tipped my head back and closed my eyes, letting the warmth rest on my face. The rush of cars taking a thousand people home. Birds overhead, or sat in trees, singing at the world. And me, here, on a sidewalk, thinking that behind me, in some back office, some minimum wage clerk was arranging for my father to disappear again.

I started digging in my bag for my new vape, so I didn't notice right away that Ray, standing by his car, was talking to somebody. A newcomer. He was thinner, paler, his stance changed as he leaned on a cane, but his bones were perfectly familiar. I'd know them in the dark. Upon them hung his darkest corduroy sports coat. He'd lost so much weight that I barely recognized him.

That wasn't the only reason.

"You shaved your moustache."

"You like it?"

I put my hand on his cheek and ran my thumb over his smooth top lip.

"I think I preferred you hairy."

"Good, because I'm planning on a beard next."

"Just a beard?"

"Yeah. Chinstrap. Like an Amish."

"Bold."

He squared his shoulders. "No more moustaches for me. Since I grew it, I've had nothing but luck."

"The wrong kind."

He caught my hand, and laced his fingers through mine.

"Not all of it," he said.

Thank You for Reading

If you enjoyed *Baby's Breath*, please consider leaving a review on Amazon.

Reviews help readers discover new stories, and they mean a great deal to independent authors like me. Even a short sentence makes a difference.

About the Author

Russell Jones is best known for his satirical nonfiction, including *The Decade in Tory*, a *Sunday Times* Bestseller, *Four Chancellors and a Funeral* and *Tories: The End of an Error.* His work has been widely shared across social media and cited in the national press for its clarity, dark humor, and incisive critique.

Before turning to writing in 2020, Russell spent three decades working as a web developer, project manager, illustrator, and designer.

Baby's Breath is his first novel.

Russell lives in Cheshire, England, with a very patient partner, an insane dog called Baxter, and two psychopathic cats who would have killed him now, if they had opposable thumbs or could get into the knife drawer. He can occasionally be found on Bluesky, where 65,000 people have chosen to read his nonsense instead of going outside with in the sunshine.

Printed in Dunstable, United Kingdom